BATH BELLES

BATH BELLES

Joan Smith

CHIVERS

British Library Cataloguing in Publication Data available

This Large Print edition published by BBC Audiobooks Ltd, Bath, 2010.
Published by arrangement with Robert Hale Ltd.

U.K. Hardcover ISBN 978 1 408 47852 3
U.K. Softcover ISBN 978 1 408 47853 0

Copyright © Joan Smith, 1986, 2009

The right of Joan Smith to be identified as author of this work has been
asserted by her in accordance with the Copyright, Designs and Patents
Act 1988

Printed and bound in Great Britain by
CPI Antony Rowe, Chippenham and Eastbourne

His lips brushed mine, lightly as a breeze. I heard a faint gasp, knew it was mine, then forgot it as his lips firmed and his arms went around me in a crushing embrace. It was unthinkable that I, the tyrant of Bath, was allowing this to happen. I made an ineffectual effort to push him away, but found my fingers weakening to water, then moving around his neck. Kissing Graham had never been like this . . .

CHAPTER ONE

'It's not very large, is it?' Mama said as she peered through her spectacles at a residence that very much resembled a doll's house. Mama was prone to understatement and euphemism.

'No wonder we had such trouble finding it,' I replied, squinting into the setting sun, whose rays slanted through the narrow spaces between our little brick house and the larger, grander ones on either side.

My sister Esther, who was only a few years beyond an interest in dolls, exclaimed, 'I think it's sweet!' Esther was seventeen, prettier than any doll, and spoiled beyond redemption. 'Just like a child's playhouse.'

'Yes, indeed, but we are not children,' I pointed out while Esther was busy showing Mama the classical pediment, and soon we went up the walk toward the door, passing through a pair of clipped yews that were the only horticultural embellishment.

Mama looked around at the neighboring homes and commented, 'The location is considered good, I believe.'

Graham Sutton, who had purchased the house, had assured me it was an easy walk to New Bond Street. The house rested on Elm Street, halfway between Mayfair and Soho,

Graham had said, though I subsequently learned it was rather closer to Soho. I took the key the lawyer had given me and opened the door. Then I felt, suddenly, the greatest reluctance to enter. Mama smiled sadly, took my arm, and said, 'It must be done sooner or later, Belle.' With her encouraging me, I went into the house where my fiance, Graham Sutton, had been murdered two years before, just a month before we were to be married.

The house, left to me in his will, was to have been our home. Two years had elapsed before my coming to claim it because of a legal tie-up. Graham's half sister from Reisling, whom he scarcely knew, had contested the will and lost. I received the house, its contents, and his carriage; his cousin and good friend Eliot Sutton was left the remainder of the estate.

I had looked forward to living with Graham in London, where he was making his way in a legal career. With him dead, however, I intended to sell the house and return to Bath with my mother and sister. I was born and raised there, and it would take more than a doll's house to pull me away. Graham's aunt, Yootha Mailer, had a summer home in Bath, where Graham and I met and eventually fell in love. I was probably the only lady in all of England for whom the sulphurous waters of the Pump Room carried the scent of romance.

The house had gaslight, but it would have been disconnected. As evening was fast

2

approaching, I said, 'We'd better scare up some candles before dark,' and plunged into the hallway. The fanlight displayed a half circle of light on the marble floor and wood paneling within. There was no gleam anywhere, but only the dullness of dust-coated surfaces. We entered timidly and turned right at the first archway into a scene of awful confusion. Every piece of furniture was askew, chairs turned upside down, books and bibelots knocked to the floor, cupboards open with their contents scattered about.

'Good gracious, what a mess!' Mama said mildly, employing her customary understatement. The place looked as though a tornado had ripped through it.

Esther exclaimed with more joy than dismay, 'We've been burgled!'

'Let's have a look at the rest of it,' I said, and darted back into the hall to find another doorway. The dining room was similarly disarranged. Going through the place room by room, I found that every single chamber was in the same state. Someone had started at the bottom and gone to the top, setting everything at odds.

'We had best call a constable,' Mama suggested.

'Yes, but first let us find a hotel room for the night,' I countered.

We had come up to London on the mail coach from Bath, taking a hired cab from the coach stop to the house, and were bone-weary. Three defenseless women walking the streets after dark seemed a bad idea. Graham had been murdered in the safety of his own home. God only knew what would befall us in this wicked city.

The 'convenient location' close to New Bond Street was little help. We turned away from New Bond in error and ended up in Soho before we finally hailed a passing hackney. When my father was alive, he had always stayed at Reddishes Hotel, and no other one occurred to any of us. We went directly to Reddishes and got booked in before calling a constable. The clerk advised us that a Bow Street Runner was what we wanted, and a Runner it was who came to our aid some hours later. A Crawler seemed a more suitable description.

Officer Harrow was a gruff, plain-spoken man who wore a ridiculous broad-brimmed white hat and a straight blue jacket. He listened to our story, showing interest only when the words 'two years ago' came up.

'You oughtn't to have waited two years to report it!'

'You oughtn't to have taken two hours to come!' I shot back swiftly, and explained the delay.

After hearing me out, he gave his verdict. 'London is full of thieves, ladies. Lock up your purses—and your daughters, ma'am,' he

4

added, with a bow to Mama. She grabbed for Esther's hand and held it tightly. 'What you've had is squatters. You're lucky there's a stick of lumber left in the place, after two years standing vacant. I've known them to carry off the doors and shutters. Oh, you can count yourself lucky you've still got the foundations. Two years! If you can figure out what's missing, send me a list, and I'll keep an eye peeled for it in my rounds of the fencing kens—that's the warehouses where they keep stolen goods—but it will have been hawked long since.'

'Where are these warehouses? We'll go ourselves,' I told him.

He cocked his head to one side and stared at my ignorance. 'That you will not, Miss Haley. Stop Hole Abbey is no place for a lady. It's the thieves' lair, you see. You wouldn't even understand a word they say, for they have their own jargon.'

'We don't know what is missing. We were never in the house before,' I pointed out.

This earned us a highly suspicious glance. 'It'd be silver plate and knickknacks they carried off first,' he said.

I remembered seeing silver candlesticks on the dining table that afternoon, and some jewelry on Graham's dresser. I mentioned this to the officer, who nibbled his quill and concluded that the burglar had been in a hurry, which seemed unlikely, considering he

5

had had two years of uninterrupted time in which to carry out his depradations.

This ignited the officer's interest to the point of offering to come around the next day and 'look us over,' as he phrased it. He had already examined Esther quite thoroughly, I can assure you.

Mama allowed, after he left, that it was 'very strange,' and that the officer was 'not terribly helpful.'

'We'll send home for some servants tomorrow and have them set the place to rights before selling,' I decided. 'Hotchkiss and Ettie will come.'

We had only planned to stay one or two nights and make the house our headquarters. As our family carriage wasn't accustomed to traveling more than ten miles, we had opted for the coach. And as we had opted for the expensive mail coach, we had taken only those seats that were absolutely necessary.

'Does that mean we'll be staying in London longer?' Esther asked hopefully. Though both Mama and I had spoiled her quite dreadfully, we had not succumbed to her pleas that we remove to the house for a Season or anything of that sort. November would hardly have been the time for it if we had. It did begin to look as though she might get a week in the city, however.

'Yes, you wretched child, we must stay,' I told her. She clapped her hands and danced in glee. Her blond curls bounced up and down, and her blue eyes sparkled.

Looking across the room to a mirror that was tarnished with age, I noticed no such enchanting reflection of myself. It wasn't the dimness of the light nor the splotching of the mirror that accounted for it, either. I looked tired and dispirited, the way I felt. Ever since Graham's death I had lived in a sort of disbelieving limbo. My hair never was gold like Esther's, nor my eyes blue, but I had allowed my brown curls to grow longer, thus robbing them of their bounce. Sorrow had taken the glow from my eyes and the roses from my cheeks. My gown hung a little slack on me, as I had lost weight. Over the past two years I had come to more closely resemble Mama than Esther. If Graham were to enter the room this minute, it would be to Esther that his eyes turned, not to me.

Esther's fluting question pulled me from my distraction. 'Can we go down and eat in the dining room?' It wasn't directed to Mama but to me. Since my father's death, his duties had somehow devolved on me. I was the one who had to make the hard decisions and receive reproachful glances. One such decision was required of me that moment. How could we go below without proper evening clothes? We had only a bandbox each, containing nightgowns and linens.

'I'm afraid not, Esther,' I said, and

explained the problem.

'It's not very grand here. We could go as we are,' she parried.

'It is rather grander than that, my dear,' Mama told her, but not without a questioning look to the tyrant.

We ate our dinner in our room, discussing what was best. 'We'll go back to Elm Street first thing in the morning,' I decided. 'We'll do what we can to set things right, then call in an estate agent and turn the house over to him to sell. I wonder what commission he will expect.'

'Grenier at home takes four percent,' Mama told me.

'Then no doubt a London agent will take five,' I concluded. 'Graham paid close to five thousand for the house. I'll ask five—two years must have given some appreciation, with our inflation rate.'

'And the agent will get two hundred and fifty guineas just for showing a few customers through your house,' Mama said wistfully. 'Six months of our income. My, it seems an easy way to earn one's money, does it not?'

'Yes, but it saves our loitering around town, you know. He will handle the whole for us. The buyer might require a mortgage—I believe the agent helps with that.'

'You could take the mortgage yourself,' Mama pointed out.

'What is the point of that?'

'Why, the house would be easier to sell if it

had a mortgage, and you'd get your money by installments, with good interest. We don't need an agent at all is what I'm saying, Belle. Why give away two hundred and fifty guineas? We could have a nice holiday in London on such a sum.'

It was a point to ponder. 'I shall put a sign in the window while we're there, at least,' I agreed.

Esther and Mama nodded conspiratorially at having cajoled me a step forward. 'And a notice in the papers,' Mama added. 'That will not cost more than a few shillings, and it will bring the house to the attention of anyone who is looking.'

'Since we are staying, could we go to the theater one night?' Esther asked eagerly. 'Please, Belle. I've never been to a real theater. We can have our gowns brought by Hotchkiss. We can call on Graham's aunt Yootha, too, and she'll invite us to a party. She is very sociable. We can go shopping on Bond Street—Graham said the house was within walking distance. Oh, it's so exciting!'

Some little excitement invaded my own being at her words. I had been so miserably depressed after Graham's death I had hardly felt like living at all, but gradually the melancholia had lifted. I had put off mourning clothes, and now, at last, I began to feel a new burgeoning of spirit within me. Yes, why not stay, if it would please little Esther? Heaven above knew she had a dull time of it at home, and so had I. Even Mama looked with lively interest to see my reaction. Poor girl, she was feeling dull, too. I wasn't the only one who had lost my mate. Papa had died only three years ago, and he had been her life. So many dire calamities befalling us had made me feel, at times, that we were all living in the Book of Job. All Mama's doings had spun around Papa's parish work at the cathedral. My father had been nothing so grand as a bishop, but only a minor ecclesiastic.

'We'll call on Yootha Mailer tomorrow, Mama, shall we?' I asked, to advise her that the tyrant was seeking her view.

'I'll drop her a note tonight' was her reply, her face split wide in a smile, and she gave another of those conspiratorial winks at Esther, as though to say, 'We've conned her.' I was not the ogre you might think, but someone had to manage the budget and the little difficulties that crop up in even the simplest of lives.

Mama was already rushing to the desk. 'See, the hotel has this letter paper right here, and a pen as well.'

They did not think to provide ink, so the letter was postponed till the next day. The reluctant tyrant was too backward to go down into the public lobby for a pot of ink. We ate what we could of the hotel fare. There was no hiding the taste of warmed-over beef, and the custard served for dessert was a block of hard stuff sitting in whey.

'A little runny,' Mama said forgivingly.

Esther and I pushed ours away and finished the meal with bread and butter. The tea was potable, and the general mood one of rejoicing.

It was odd that, having gone at last to the house where Graham had been killed, I should now begin to push him to the back of my mind and feel something like joy and excitement return to my life. A little trip will often drive away the blue devils. I should not have waited so long to get out again into the world. When a young lady is staring at the windy side of twenty, she hasn't time to dawdle. Was it possible my mind had begun to consider the unthinkable—that I might yet find someone to usurp Graham's place in my heart?

The next morning, unwilling to waste a minute before getting into the social whirl, Mama asked the maid for ink and wrote her note to Yootha Mailer before taking breakfast. I used the time to write my sale notice for the newspapers and my letter home to Hotchkiss and Ettie, and I had them all sent off by a hotel page. This done, we called a hackney to deliver us once more to Elm Street.

Having been astonished by the small size of the house the day before, I was agreeably surprised to find it was larger than I remembered. The bright sun striking its facade

11

removed the previous day's gloom and made it appear prettier. The doorway was elegant, and the facade had leaded windows on either side of the door. It was three stories high—too tall for anything of symmetry or balance, but it was in decent repair. Nothing, alas, had changed within. The confusion was still there waiting for us, but it was easier to face in the morning than at the end of a long trip. We put off our pelisses, tucked tea towels into our waistbands, and got to work.

'I wonder where it happened,' Esther remarked as we put the cushions back on the sofa and arranged the toss pillows on top of them. The sofa was a pale blue satin, striped with a deeper blue and yellow. The velvet toss pillows were gold, to match the draperies. Graham had selected all this elegance, consulting with me on colors and styles.

'Right here, I expect,' I said. 'His body was found on the sofa.' My voice was hard and cold, to prevent it from trembling at the awful picture that darted into my head of poor Graham stretched out, perhaps on the very velvet pillow I held in my hands, and clutched to my breast.

Esther peered around at the sofa and carpet. Her voice was sepulchral. 'I wonder if there's any blood,' she said.

'Not likely, Esther. A victim of strangulation doesn't bleed, as far as I know.' The police assumed Graham had been strangled by human hands, as no rope or cord was left behind. The motive was called robbery. His money purse was missing, but a small diamond tie pin was left intact. How much cash would a struggling young solicitor carry with him? Surely not enough that he would defend it with his life. Graham would have, though. He was like that. The injustice of it would have caused him to fight to the death. It was not mere chance that had led him to the study of the law.

'Who do you think killed him?' Esther asked as she went on fitting some drawers into a small wall table.

'A person or persons unknown,' I said grimly. I really didn't want to know more or to think about it at all. Some criminal had killed a good, honorable man and gotten clean away. It was done, and no good could come from harking back to it. The police had investigated thoroughly, Yootha had said, and had learned nothing.

'Esther, come and help me in the kitchen,' Mama said, but her worried voice revealed her reasoning. She didn't want me reminded unnecessarily of the past. Esther would have a peal rung over her for discussing the murder. As though I could help thinking the same thoughts myself!

We got the living and dining rooms and a bedroom each put to rights by noon and were ready for lunch. We set off in the proper direction to reach New Bond Street, where we made our meal at a small restaurant. I was in charge of decisions for us all, and my next decision was that henceforth we would eat at the house. Meals out were not only unappetizing and expensive, but also inconvenient. We shopped for food, and then I remembered to go and have the gas turned on. We returned to Elm Street, already finding the little brick house familiar and welcoming after the hour spent amid the busy throng of London.

During the afternoon we arranged our creature comforts around us in the house, moving lamps and small tables and so on to suit us. We put away the food when it was delivered and were just lighting candles to ward off the early dark of November when the man from the gas company came to connect us. We enjoyed our first meal there by gaslight, and we felt very modern and citified, turning the knobs to make it as bright as daylight till the tyrant decided we were wasting expensive gas and turned them down to a less harsh glare.

Building a fire in the stove proved difficult. I had seen the servants light the grate often enough that I knew what should be done, but the thing was harder to accomplish in a closed stove. In the end we ate cold ham with bread and cheese in the saloon and heated our tea kettle on the hob while Esther made toast on a long fork. It was cozy, like a picnic, eating around the fire with an unusual quantity of traffic streaming past a few yards beyond. For the first dozen carriages we ran to look out the window, but in the end we became blase about the clatter and the bobbing lights. We drew the curtains and settled in to read the papers we had picked up while shopping. Our advertisement had not been inserted yet.

'I shall put my sign in the window,' I decided, and drew one up to look as official and businesslike as my wobbly print could make it. That it be legible from the street was the important point. 'House for Sale. Inquire within' was all I wrote.

Meanwhile, Esther had discovered the entertainment page of the paper and was busy regaling us with all manner of divertissements open to Londoners and tourists. There were plays and concerts, operas and ballets, lectures, and public dances enough to satisfy the entire population of London. Esther soon decided that what suited a clutch of unescorted ladies from Bath was a comedy to be played for a week at the Haymarket Theatre. She received tentative agreement, pending arrival of our servants with our clothes and approval from Yootha Mailer, who was to be our social arbiter.

I spent close to an hour checking the real estate columns to determine if the price we planned to ask for our house was fair. I couldn't make head or tail of the prices demanded, but I assumed that the reason one eight-room house was going for seven thousand guineas and another for four must have to do with location. As there was nothing 'with gas' under five, I decided to ask six and judge by my first customer's face if he thought me insane or a flat.

With no candles shrinking to alert us to the hours' passing, we stayed up till midnight. The gaslight was remarkable, turning night to day. Mama and I repaired a rent made in the saloon draperies when they were torn from their tracks, while we all discussed the vandalization of the house.

'It seems like spite, plain and simple,' Mama said 'I don't believe a single thing was stolen. The silver candlesticks are still here, and a very fine silver tea service. You'll want to take that home, Belle.' She went on to name other easily removable objects that hadn't been pilfered.

'Graham's jewelry box has in it everything I remember seeing him wear, too,' I agreed. 'Except his diamond stickpin, and the lawyer said he will be sending over a package tomorrow with the items he was wearing when . . .' I swallowed down a lump, and Mama spoke up to rescue me.

'That is an odd sort of thief,' she opined.

'It was just hooligans. I'm grateful they didn't do more mischief while they were about

16

it—break dishes and mirrors and windows, I mean.'

'How do you think they got in?' Esther asked idly. 'You had to unlock the door, Belle, and there were no windows broken, were there?'

I jumped up in alarm to double-check. 'I didn't notice any!'

'There were none broken. They were all closed and locked. He must have had a key,' Mama announced. She was a good housekeeper and noticed such things. I stopped in my tracks.

'He might have gotten in through the cellar,' Esther suggested. Comforting thought!

There was nothing for it but to take a candle to the cellar and check. I was thankful we did, despite the frightening trip into the black bowels, for there, where it was not easily seen, was a window wide open to the elements, both criminal and climatic. The wrongdoer had obviously crept in there and gone up the stairs and into the pantry. There was no lock on the pantry door. We locked the basement window, propped a chair under the handle of the pantry door, and returned to the saloon, carrying two dusty bottles of wine from Graham's well-stocked cellar.

'It's odd Graham would have left that window unlocked when everything else was closed properly,' Mama said.

'Especially as it exposed his wine cellar to

17

the cold,' I agreed. Graham was a bit of a fanatic about his wine.

'What I wonder is how the thief ever discovered it,' Esther mused.

'Very true,' Mama nodded. 'The back yard has no easy access from the street. There is that pretty bit of iron fence enclosing the yard. Fairly high, and with a spiked top. It is certainly odd.'

'Officer Harrow is right,' I said. 'London is full of thieves.' He was supposed to have dropped around earlier, but I doubted we'd ever see him.

'Yet after the whole two years, nothing much is missing, so far as we can see,' Mama pointed out, frowning over the drapery, her needle poised for action. 'It certainly is odd.'

So it was, and we were fortunate no other marauder had discovered the secret. We agreed we must keep all doors and windows locked when we were out of the house and left it at that.

When we finally went upstairs to bed I found it impossible to occupy the master bedroom, which had been chosen as mine. Graham had done it up in dusky blue and white, according to my wishes. The canopy and drapes were blue, the carpet and walls white with some blue and gold ornaments. His things were laid out there as if he might walk in the door any moment and smile at me. I could almost imagine him coming. I felt the old

18

excitement, aggravated now by a shivering chill. So tall, so handsome—or so he seemed to me. He had the loveliest chestnut hair, just touched with a natural wave. My favorite of Graham's features was his noble brow. It was high and clear, with the hair growing to a widow's peak in front.

I picked up his silver-backed brush, touched the comb with one of his hairs still on it. The blue jacket he must have worn to work that day was still slung over the back of a chair. The servants should have tidied up before leaving. I knew from the lawyer that the two servants had been paid and sent off, his horses sold, and other such exigent matters attended to. But no one had packed his clothes and personal effects. It would be for me to do.

I'd have Hotchkiss make up a bundle of anything he didn't want and give it to charity. Some few mementos I would keep—Graham's watch, perhaps, or a bit of jewelry. I drew open the drawer of his desk and saw bound up in blue ribbons my letters to him, as his to me were in my desk at home. The oval miniature I had given him of a young Belle Haley was there on his desk where he could look at it while he wrote to me, as he mentioned once in a letter he did. It was an eerie sensation, almost like having a last chance to talk to Graham. I said what one must say in a final conversation. Goodbye, dear Graham. I love you. Then I quietly closed the door and met

19

Mama, come to see if I was in tears.

'Go to bed, Mama. It's very late,' I said.

'Are you . . . all right, Belle?' she asked.

'I'm fine. Graham wouldn't want me to cry willow forever, but I shall sleep in the other room. I was just—saying goodbye to him.'

'It's for the best, dear,' she consoled, and patted my shoulder.

I kissed her cheek and went to the rose room at the end of the hall. This room facing the street was noisy, even past midnight. How could people live amid such bustle? Did folks never settle down in London? It was impossible not to think how things would have been had Graham lived. I would be lying with him in that lovely blue canopied bed. By now, a child might be sleeping in another room. But it was not to be, so I would sell the house, let some other lady fill up the nursery here, and get on with a different life for myself back home at Bath. Oh, but what a hollow, meaningless life it was without Graham!

CHAPTER TWO

At Bath we considered ourselves early risers, but we were not in the habit of entertaining callers at such an early hour as nine o'clock. That was the time our first caller arrived at Elm Street. A respectable-looking woman in a navy pelisse with sable trim stood on the doorstep. She had determined that the house was for sale and expressed an interest in seeing it. I didn't want to let her get away, yet to take her on a tour when Mama and Esther were still making toast over the coals in the saloon grate was obviously undesirable.

'If you could come back in an hour . . . I suggested. She tossed her head and sniffed. 'There are plenty of homes for sale. If you're not interested . . .'

I ground my teeth at her lofty manner and said, 'Do come in.' She entered, looking all around at the windows, uncleaned for upwards of two years, ran her finger over dusty window ledges, opened cupboards and found their doors poorly hung or requiring oil, or the shelves within badly spaced. With *tsks* of annoyance from the customer and disjointed explanations from myself, the tour continued to bedrooms with unmade beds, everything 'so terribly small,' halls 'pitch black,' stairways 'dangerously steep.' I came to appreciate my mother's manner of description that morning.

And after it was all over the woman had the gall to say, 'I am not really looking for a house at the moment.'

'Then why are you here?' I demanded, eyes flashing.

'I am your next-door neighbor,' she said, as though that gave her carte blanche to barge in at dawn, disturb our breakfast, and disparage

21

everything. 'Mrs Seymour. My husband and I live in the large house on the corner. We have often mentioned removing to a smaller place now that the children have left home. This spot is so handy it seemed worth a look, though of course it is much too small and really in very bad repair.'

'The size, at least, must have been apparent before you entered,' I pointed out. She simpered and looked around the room once more.

She cleared her throat and said, 'Is this the room where—it happened?'

I knew perfectly well what she meant, but decided to make her confess her morbid and ill-bred curiosity. 'Where what happened?'

'Ah, you do not know the house's history, Miss Haley. The fact of the matter is a man was murdered here!' She looked triumphant at telling me so. She thought I'd bought the house unawares and she was thrilled to point out my folly. 'Yes, in this very room, I fancy. The papers said the saloon, at least. A very grisly business it was, too. There was some theft involved—a huge sum of money the man had embezzled.'

I gave her an icy stare. 'You are mistaken. Mr Sutton was robbed; he had stolen nothing. I am quite aware of the matter. And as you were only interested in looking, Mrs Seymour, perhaps you will want to leave now. I expect your husband is waiting for his breakfast. I know I am ready for mine.'

She looked at the kettle boiling on the hob, the plates on the sofa table, shook her head in weary disdain, and left. She was about as impressed with our housekeeping as we were with her manners.

The nerve of that creature!' I exclaimed.

'I thought her very curious—vulgarly so,' Mama said mildly.

Esther put a piece of bread on the fork and resumed making our breakfast. When another woman appeared at the door half an hour later, with no evidence of a carriage, I took for granted she was another nosy neighbor. She confessed as much on the doorstep. She lived on our other side.

'I'm Mrs George,' she said 'I noticed you have the house up for sale.'

'Yes, are you in the market for a very small house in some disrepair, ma'am?' I asked coolly before inviting her in.

'Oh, no, I only came over to get acquainted, to see if I could be of any help. It's nice to have someone to point out the shops nearby, and so on.'

My short temper had led me into unintentional rudeness. As I let her in I noticed that she was altogether a better class of person than Mrs Seymour, which is not to say that she was above a few prying questions as to where 'it' happened. Of course, she didn't know of my relationship with Graham or how painful it was to speak of it. During the course of our conversation Mama mentioned that someone had gotten in and made a mess of the house.

'Is that what he was up to?' Mrs George asked. 'My daughter had some notion it was ghosts. They will often haunt a place where there has been a violent death,' she informed us with perfect seriousness. 'I have seen the lights moving about in here at night. I sent off for a constable the first time, but by the time he came the ghost had left. That was just after poor Mr Sutton was killed. Then the lights did not appear again till just recently. One night about a week ago I saw the light. I mentioned it to my husband, but he said it was none of my business; it was probably the new owner having a look around. As if the owner would not have entered by the front door! I tell you no one did, for my sewing corner gives a very clear view of your door. And the ghost didn't leave by the front door, either. I kept a sharp eye, and no one came out, even after the lights vanished.'

'A week ago, you say—and no lights since?' I asked.

'Not a one. And I kept an eye peeled.'

'That is odd,' Mama allowed, with a little frown.

Mrs George nodded her head and said, 'Perhaps it was someone looking for the money.'

24

I assumed she had been gossiping with Mrs Seymour and prepared to give her a setdown. 'Mr Sutton was not a thief! He was the victim.'

'But there was talk at the time that he had gotten hold of some huge sum of money—I don't know exactly what it was. It wasn't in the papers, but there were police officers searching the house for money—a whole bag of it. They asked me if I had seen anything of it, but I could not learn from them how that nice Mr Sutton came to have such a sum. It stands to reason he was not rich, buying a tiny little place like this for his wife. He was to have been married very soon.'

She didn't leap to the conclusion that I was to have been the bride, and I saw no reason to tell her. My mind was occupied with her more interesting statements. She soon rose to leave and said she hoped we could all come to call on her after we had settled in.

'Or will you be staying at all?' she asked, remembering the sign in the window.

It began to seem we might be staying longer than we had planned. I meant to discover what this bag of money was that Graham was supposed to have had the night he was murdered.

When we were alone again, Esther said, 'What can it mean?'

'It must have something to do with his legal business,' I decided. 'I thought it odd anyone would kill him only for the contents of his purse.'

'And leave his little diamond stickpin behind, too,' Mama reminded me.

'Graham had no partner—there is no one to ask.'

Mama was frowning, biting her bottom lip. 'If the man came back several times and came again just last week, Belle, it looks as though he did not *get* the money,' she pointed out.

I felt a moment's weakness from fright, but it was the tyrant's job to be in charge, so I assumed a bold front. 'How nice! Then we can look forward to more visits from him. I shall have the locks changed this very day. We shan't sleep tonight in a house without safe locks.'

'Mrs George said he didn't use the door,' Esther reminded me.

'Mrs George is a goose. He used the back door—or that cellar window. We'll have the locks changed anyway, and a bolt put on the cellar door as well.'

After a frowning pause, Mama said, 'I do wish Hotchkiss were here.'

I pointed out that Hotchkiss would not even have my letter yet and couldn't reasonably be expected for a few days. 'I'm going down to Bond Street this minute to see if I can find a locksmith.'

'I'll go with you,' Esther volunteered eagerly.

Mama blanched and shrieked, 'I'm not

staying here alone!'

'We cannot all go and leave the place empty. Someone might come to see the house,' I reminded them. 'I'll stay.'

'Not alone, Belle,' Mama objected. 'There is no saying all the customers will be ladies.'

'Very true. We haven't had a real lady so far,' I said, but of course it was a gentleman caller she feared, and I had no wish to tour the place alone with a gentleman. 'We'll all go together this afternoon. It won't take more than an hour.'

Just after we got the breakfast debris cleared away, we heard a third tap at the door. Things move quickly in the city. At home, the Barrows had their house up for a month before they had a caller. It was Esther who pranced to the door, gold curls bouncing, when she spotted the handsome black carriage in the street and the elegant, many-caped greatcoat emerging from it.

'This is Mr Desmond,' she said, showing him in. 'He wants to see the house.'

Why? was the first thing that popped into my head. A gentleman who drove that elegant carriage outside our door and who emanated such a strong air of wealth and fashion did not belong in this toy house on Elm Street. He belonged in a mansion in the very heart of fashionable London. He was exceedingly handsome in a dashing way that was new to me, and to Esther, too, to judge from her

27

adoring gaze. The thing that set Mr Desmond apart from Bath gentlemen had to do with his manner as well, his open way of appraising us all, not trying to hide his curiosity; yet the manner was friendly enough. Short, dark hair sat smoothly on a well-sculpted head. The word 'sculpted' suited his entire body, for it was of ideal proportions. The carving of the face was particularly fine, from the high cheekbones and strong jaw to the slightly sensuous lips. It was his liveliness and a pair of dancing dark eyes that removed the look of a Grecian statue. Those bold eyes, that mobile expression, had nothing to do with cold marble. A flirtatious smile began and then subsided as his glance flitted from Esther to me to Mama.

The vision opened its lips, and a deep, melodious voice spoke. 'Good morning, ladies. I hope I haven't dropped in at an inconvenient hour. When will it be best for me to return and tour the house?'

'Now!' I said swiftly. 'You may as well look now, Mr Desmond. We plan to go out this afternoon.' I explained, but in a voice suffering from discomposure, that we had just arrived without servants and that the place wanted a good cleaning.

'That suits me.' He removed his outer coat, revealing a blue jacket exquisitely molded to broad shoulders. Sparkling linen and a discreetly patterned waistcoat were also displayed.

Something about this elegant Adonis robbed me of my wits. Instead of taking his coat and getting down to business, I just went on looking and smiling back at him, for his flickering gaze had finally settled on me. Only Mama proved immune to the man's charm. She said, 'The house is small.'

'Yes, I can see that,' he agreed, looking about at the little toy saloon.

'It would not do for a large family,' she added. She has the country habit of wanting to know all about any stranger met by chance. I found myself listening with keen interest for his reply. I also found myself wondering about the mischievous sparkle that suddenly invaded his eyes.

'It is not wanted for a family,' he said blandly.

This speech quite disconcerted me for about thirty seconds. Within half a minute, though, I realized what had brought this fashionable buck to my door. He was searching out a love nest for his mistress! My first reaction was revulsion that the house Graham had bought for us should be put to such a base use. He recognized the accusation in my stare and tried to smile it away.

'Who is the tour mistress?' he asked. I felt it was more than coincidence that he had chosen the word *mistress*. There was a certain playful quality in the way he said it. I was tempted to turn him out the door, but reason prevailed. What did it matter now? If he had the money and wanted the house, that was all that concerned me.

'Belle?' Mama said, calling me to my duty.

'I'll conduct the tour,' I said briskly.

Mama and Esther remained seated, which meant I was to be allowed to accompany Mr Desmond alone. I was glad they were there within shouting distance all the same.

'This is the saloon,' I began. 'A rather nice marble fireplace.'

'Not Adam, though,' he pointed out.

'Perhaps not. Pretty leaded windows,' I continued, nodding at them. He gazed with mild interest at these treats.

'The room is rather small. Do you happen to know the dimensions?' he asked.

'You could pace it out,' Mama said. 'A tall man's stride is about a yard.'

'That would be rather difficult . . .' I objected. The difficulty arose from the fact that furniture occupied both ends of the room: sofas at one end, a heavy highboy at the other.

Undeterred, Mr Desmond wedged himself in at the end of the sofa and paced the room, squeezing his long leg in between the highboy and a bookcase when he got to the far end. 'I make it about six yards,' he announced. 'And roughly five wide. Does the place come furnished?'

'If you like. Or I can sell the furniture

separately—either way,' I said.

'I'd like to keep that highboy, Belle,' Mama said. 'It would look fine in our own saloon at Bath. So much nicer than the great ugly cupboard we have there.'

'Ah, you're from Bath!' Mr Desmond exclaimed. 'That would explain your beautiful complexions. I spent a week at Bath one day.'

Mama and Esther exchanged a perplexed frown while Mr Desmond honored me with a quizzing smile, to confirm that I had properly interpreted his opinion of dull Bath.

'What price are you asking?' was his next question.

Six thousand pounds,' I suggested tentatively, watching to gauge his response.

He nodded, neither delighted, dismayed, nor surprised, and said, 'May I see the bedchambers?'

'Yes, they're upstairs,' I said, and we walked from the safety of the saloon.

'A novel idea,' I heard him say in a soft voice as he paced behind me. 'And—just a suggestion, Miss Haley—firm up your tone when you give the price. That doubtful glance is an invitation to the unscrupulous purchaser to haggle you down. What would you really take?'

'Six thousand pounds,' I said much more firmly.

'That's better!' he complimented.

I was overly conscious of him behind me,

following me up the stairs, down the hall. I was on pins and needles waiting for him to say or do something outrageous, but he just walked into each chamber, looked all around at ceilings, windows, wainscoting, personal clutter. I saved the master bedroom for the last, as it was the finest. A picture popped into my head of Mr Desmond's mistress lounging at her ease in Graham's bed. She was a voluptuous blonde in a white lace peignoir. I disliked the image intensely. 'No one using the master bedroom?' he asked.

'Not at the moment, but it would do equally well for a mistress's bedchamber, don't you think?' I gave him a bright, impersonal smile.

The sparkle from his laughing eye only hit me at an angle as he turned away to hide his face. Even the partial view made me realize I had strayed into suggestive waters. 'Yes, indeed. What has sex to do with a bedchamber, after all?' He laughed lightly and strolled over to punch the mattress with his fists. 'This is a demmed hard mattress.'

'Mattresses can easily be changed.'

'Oh, I like a good firm mattress. I'm an active—er, sleeper.'

I refused to be bullied into embarrassment by this creature, who was trying his best to discomfort me. 'There is some interesting carving on the wooden fireplace,' I pointed out. He walked to it and ran his fingers over the flowers and birds. 'This also is not the

32

work of Adam,' I said, for him.

'Nor of Grinling Gibbons either, though it's not too crudely done,' he allowed. He turned back and surveyed the room at some length. 'This is not bad.'

'I think she'll like,' I said.

He picked up on it at once. 'She?'

'Your—your wife,' I said, coloring briskly.

'Ah, yes, my wife, of course. She would no doubt like it immensely, if she existed.'

I showed not an iota of interest in his marital status, though I would relay my finding to Esther. 'It would be ideal for a bachelor as well,' I replied.

'Ideal? It hardly complies with the highest perfection to be attained in bedchambers, but it is not bad. May I see the attic? Above the bedrooms, I expect?' he asked archly.

'Very likely. I haven't been to the attic yet myself. I dread to think what state it is in.'

We went along the hall to the attic stairs. The most notable thing about the attic was that it was extremely cold. Mr Desmond noticed my shiver and immediately drew off his jacket and hung it over my shoulders. The size of his shoulders was not much diminished nor the shape much changed by the removal of the jacket. The face, though, took on a bolder expression.

'That's not at all necessary. I can get a shawl,' I protested. But I was grateful for its warmth.

33

'Aren't you afraid I'd pilfer from your attic if you left me alone?' he joked.

'I doubt you could get any of those trunks into your pocket.' There wasn't much but three trunks up there.

'Who knows what might be in them? Bags of gold, for all we know.' As he spoke he went forward and tried the lids. They were all locked.

'I hardly think so!' What an odd coincidence that he should name a bag of gold—just what Graham was supposed to have stolen. But it was only a coincidence; there was no knowing look from him.

When we returned below I made sure to give him back his jacket before entering the saloon, in case Mama would think it overly familiar of me to have accepted it. It was just at the door of the master bedroom that I returned it.

'Would you mind holding it?' he asked. 'I can hardly squeak into it without my valet.'

I found myself holding Mr Desmond's jacket while he slid his arms into it. Without thinking what I was about, I automatically lifted my hand and eased out a crease while he pulled it down in front. When I realized what I was doing I pulled my hand away as if he were on fire. 'Why, thank you, Miss Haley,' he said over his shoulder. 'My valet and I are grateful to you. We have our sartorial reputation to maintain. Pipp would be furious with me if I

34

appeared in public in wrinkles.' He spoke lightly.

I found myself smiling at this bold city gentleman, who smiled back readily in a way that set my blood racing. I felt the urge to flee back downstairs to safety. 'Shall we go down and discuss the sale?' I suggested. 'Over a glass of sherry, perhaps . . .'

'By all means, but if you hope to get me tipsy and coerce an offer to purchase from me, I must warn you, you'll look no how. I holds my liquor like a gentle mort. I bet a vicar's daughter don't.' On this speech he took my arm, and we soon entered the saloon in a fit of laughter over some foolishness or other.

It would be hard to say who was more astonished—Mama or Esther. Their startled faces brought us back to propriety with a thump. Mr Desmond took charge of the conversation in a brisk, businesslike manner.

'I would like to bring a builder along to go over the place thoroughly before making an offer,' he said. 'To see if the building is structurally sound, you know. I don't want to get into the expense of having to put on a new roof or shore up crumbling walls.'

'Oh, it is not that bad, Mr Desmond!' Mama assured him. 'The windows are drafty, to be sure, and the closet doors poorly hung, but the walls are not *crumbling*.'

'But you will have no objection to my bringing a builder?' he repeated.

'None at all,' I said hastily, lest he take the idea we were trying to hide some flaw.

'Tomorrow, say, at eleven o'clock?' he asked. He pulled out a little appointment book, which gave me the notion he was a very busy man of affairs. But when I got a peek over his shoulder I saw his appointments were not so serious as that. It was 'Tattersall's, settling up day,' 'Lunch with Boo at Whites,' 'Dinner and rout party, Lady Higgins,' and similar important matters that filled his page. 'Miss Haley—check house' was squeezed in between Tattersall's and lunch with Boo.

There was no opportunity to relay Mr Desmond's state of single blessedness to Mama, so she instituted a quiz herself. 'Will your wife also come to see the house?' she asked, slyly innocent.

'As I was telling your daughter, ma'am, I don't have a wife yet.' Esther pursed her lips and smiled, but fortunately Mr Desmond was looking at me at the time.

'The house is a good size for a bachelor, yet large enough that a young family could stay on till their nursery had two or three youngsters in it,' Mama said. 'Is it handy to your place of work, Mr Desmond?' she continued.

'Fairly close. I work at the Royal Exchange,' he answered, which did not enlighten us much. 'You ladies are removing from London entirely, are you?'

'We never lived here,' Mama said. 'We hail

36

from Bath—remember I mentioned it. This is the first time my daughters have ever been to London. My elder'—and she nodded at me— 'inherited the house, but we shan't live in it.'

Mr Desmond settled in to humor her. 'I think you would like London. Bath is not far— you could use the house for the Season, at least.'

Such high flights of sophistication were miles above us. Mama looked at him as if he were a Bedlamite. 'Not far! It took *two days* to get here! As to liking London, it is no such thing. We have no opinion of it, I assure you. We just want to get our money and bolt back home.'

When Mr Desmond recovered from her outburst, he admitted mildly that Bath was 'nice.' 'Did something in particular occur to give you this distaste for London?' he asked politely.

'You wouldn't believe the state this place was in when we got here,' she began. 'A house standing empty invites trouble, of course. A vandal got in and turned the place upside down.'

You would think Mr Desmond had already bought the place, to see the wild leap of interest in his eyes. 'Tell me about it!'

I jumped in to quiet his fears that the neighborhood was a low one, prone to these senseless attacks. 'He did no damage to the house. It was just a prank—the furniture

37

hauled about, you know, but no real damage.'

'That's a pity. An unpleasant shock for you. Did the police have any word on the culprit?'

'Mrs George thinks it was a ghost,' Esther said, her eyes wide with fear.

Mr Desmond tossed me a quick look to see if she was joking. When he determined that she was as witless as she sounded, he said with admirably firm lips, 'If the candle didn't burn blue, then it could not have been a ghost.'

'That's what I thought,' she nodded.

'About the police, Mrs Haley . . .' he continued, looking to Mama for common sense.

She was happy to vent her opinion of city law enforcement. 'They were no help at all,' she assured him, and she related our experiences at the hands of Officer Harrow. 'And he didn't come around either, Belle, as he promised he would, to check us out. The Bow Street Crawler, Belle calls him.'

'I'm surprised. Bow Street has an excellent reputation,' Mr Desmond said mildly. 'Do you suppose there was any particular reason why someone broke in? I mean, as nothing was taken—if it had been a cove on the ken lay, he'd have snaffled the . . .' He became aware that he had lost us. 'Housebreakers usually steal things,' he interpreted.

Before Mama could begin the tale of Graham's death, I spoke up. 'No, Officer Harrow thinks it was just pranksters, because

38

the house was empty. An invitation to them, really. I daresay a couple of bucks got in and had a party.'

'Why did you wait so long before disposing of the house?' was his next question.

'It was tied up in litigation,' I said briefly.

He finished his sherry, and I accompanied him to the front door to remind him of the appointment the next morning.

'I'll be here—but I still think you should keep the house, Miss Haley, even if you're not getting married.' He set his curled beaver on at a jaunty angle, picked up his gloves and cane, and left.

'Even if you're not getting married.' How did he know that? Surely I hadn't told him. No, of course I hadn't. I went back to the saloon, where Esther was praising Mr Desmond to Mama. 'What were the two of you laughing about when you came downstairs, Belle?' she asked.

'Nothing—I don't remember. Mama, did we tell Mr Desmond I was to have been married?'

'No, dear, we didn't. Did he seem to take a shine to you?'

'No, but he mentioned my not getting married. And upstairs he said something about Papa being a clergyman.'

'He must have heard of your father,' she decided. 'And that would explain how he knew about your not getting married.'

But I knew Mr Desmond, a city buck, had

39

never heard of a minor clergyman in Bath. That wasn't it. It was conceivable he knew Yootha Mailer. That was the only way he could possibly have heard of me and Graham.

'Do you want to go to the locksmith now?' Esther asked, eager to return to Bond Street.

We decided to do it while there was a lull in our customers, and while we were out we decided to tackle one more restaurant for lunch. We had better luck than before; the chicken was quite tasty. The locksmith agreed to come that afternoon and make us safe. So far as we could tell, no one had made free of the house during our absence. The only thing of interest was that the fire in the grate had gone out, and we had to rebuild it. The obstinate thing petered out in a fog of smoke within minutes.

Officer Harrow finally came, as he had promised. When he saw the locksmith at work he didn't bother with any investigation.

'That's the ticket. New locks,' he complimented us.

He was a very inferior officer of the law, but he built us a roaring fire in about two minutes and accepted a glass of sherry in payment.

'If you have any further difficulties, ladies, just give us a call at Bow Street. Always willing to oblige.'

He clamped his wide-brimmed hat on his head and went out whistling. I didn't think we would have further need of Officer Harrow.

He was useless as a policeman, and I had learned his trick for getting the fire blazing. He stuffed crushed newspapers under the grate. There was a good stack of old newspapers in a brass basket by the hearth. I had planned to throw them out, but would keep them.

CHAPTER THREE

Mrs Mailer, Graham's Aunt Yootha, came to call around four. We had the habit of calling her Aunt Yootha behind her back, as we so often heard Graham do, but to her face she is Mrs Mailer. We had known her as Miss Almont, Mrs Dunne, Mrs Arnold, and most recently as Mrs Mailer. She had three husbands in the grave and was hard at work looking for a fourth. I expected she would find one too, for she was attractive somehow, without actually being pretty. Her hair was a brindled shade, but always fashionably styled. Liveliness was her chief attraction and lent some charm to her ordinary appearance. It was impossible not to like Yootha, and equally impossible to admire her, for her concerns were all selfish and frivolous.

What endeared her to me in particular was that she was always so kind to Graham. He ran quite tame at her house in Bath, where I met

41

him, and his letters told me he was every bit as welcome at Berkeley Square in London.

We were alerted to her call by a banging on the wood of the front door. The brass acorn knocker was awaiting the arrival of Hotchkiss, who would return it to its rightful place. Esther darted to answer the knock.

Mrs Mailer brought a whiff of London glamour in with her. A delightful confection of ostrich feathers and satin ribbons adorned her head, adding a needed half foot or so to her diminutive size. She had on a sable-trimmed pelisse, a strikingly handsome brown crepe gown beneath, and a set of heavy gold chains and ear buttons.

'I got your note and came dashing over immediately,' she exclaimed, embracing Mama like a long-lost sister. Esther and I each received a peck on the cheek before she was invited to draw a chair closer to the grate. Harrow's blazing fire was welcome in these dark, cold days. 'Whatever possessed you to put the house up for sale, Belle?' she asked me.

'Oh, you've seen my sign.' I smiled, for we hadn't mentioned selling to her.

'Sign? No, I didn't see a sign.'

'How did you know, then?'

'I heard it somewhere or other. I believe Eliot was by and saw it. Graham's cousin, you know. But you are foolish to sell the place. You ought to give these lasses a Season, Mrs

Haley,' she said, turning to address Mama.

'They are not interested in that,' Mama said firmly.

Esther objected noisily. 'I *am* interested!'

'And well you might be, naughty puss.' Mrs Mailer smiled. 'So pretty, like a little china doll. This one takes up where Helen of Troy leaves off. And with the addition to their dowry of this place, your daughters are entirely eligible for presentation, in a small way.'

My nose was put out of joint by this heaping of praise on Esther without a drop for myself. It wasn't many years ago that Yootha had hailed me as the year's new Incomparable.

'That is Belle's money,' Mama pointed out. 'And in any case, we are not properly connected to carry out a presentation.'

'I would be happy to present the pair of them. I should love it. No daughters of my own—there is nothing I would prefer to presenting them. Find you both good partis too, I guarantee,' she said, tapping her knee with her gloves.

'Don't encourage the child,' I implored her. 'Never mind finding us partis—find us a buyer, Mrs Mailer.'

She cocked her head to one side and frowned. 'That would be difficult—the place is so small. I can't imagine what maggot Graham got in his noggin to buy you this toy box when he had every intention of filling a nursery. Most people would require more space.'

43

'We have already had a few lookers,' Mama told her. 'We have a man coming back for the second time tomorrow, bringing a builder. That augurs a serious interest.'

Mrs Mailer looked alert. 'What price are you asking?'

I told her and asked her opinion. 'High, but then you want to ask the moon and you might get a few stars. Certainly, ask six thousand, but be prepared to take five.'

What was uppermost in my mind all the time now was to learn about the money Graham was supposed to have had when he was killed. I managed to get the question out without choking over the word *'killed'*.

She nodded her head knowingly. 'The insurance money. Yes, I knew about it but could not trouble you with the story at the time, Belle, for you were so terribly depressed and disturbed. There is no great mystery in it, after all. I meant to tell you one day. It was insurance money Graham had, money belonging to Lloyd's of London.'

'The neighbors implied he had stolen it,' I told her.

'Bah, Nosy Parker neighbors, what do they know? I was directly involved, Belle, and Graham was no more stealing it than you were. It happened like this. I had my emerald necklace insured with Lloyd's for twenty-five thousand guineas. The one Mr Arnold gave me, dear Horace, so very generous,' she added

44

contentedly. 'It was stolen, and I applied to the agent for the claim money.'

Esther's eyes grew wide, and she said, 'You mean Graham had as much as twenty-five thousand guineas?'

'No, my pet, not that much. The agent from Lloyd's was an extremely nasty man. He implied, though he did not dare to actually say it, that I had arranged the theft myself to get the claim money. He could not prove it, of course, for it was an infamous lie. It happened I had lost a ring a year before and gotten insurance money for it, but it wasn't the same agent that time. The agent dragged his heels about paying for the necklace, and eventually he got lucky. Some criminal got in touch with him and offered to get him back the necklace for a fraction of its worth. Ten thousand pounds in banknotes was the price the insurance agent had to come up with. They struck some bargain to have the necklace returned in a gin mill in Long Acre in exchange for the ten thousand. I knew all about it and told Graham. Graham conceived the foolish notion of loitering about behind a fence or some such thing, and he followed the man who got the money from the agent. He knocked him out, grabbed the bag of money from him, and ran home—here, to this very house. He meant to return it to Lloyd's, you see, but he never could do it. The villain managed to follow him home and killed him.

He snatched up the money and got clean away. They never caught him. That is why dear Graham was murdered. I felt so awfully guilty, though I told him a dozen times not to involve himself, and Eliot told him the same thing. Graham and Eliot were very close friends— well, first cousins. Eliot would have been killed as well, but fortunately he had a horse running somewhere that day and wasn't in town. What was it to Graham if Lloyd's had to pay up for my necklace? That is what we pay them for. But you know Graham,' she finished sadly.

'How do you know all this if Graham was dead before he could tell anyone what happened?' I asked.

'We pieced the story together from what we knew. The insurance agent told me about the exchange he had arranged—to pacify me, I daresay. I had threatened to hire a solicitor. I knew Graham planned to intercept the man with the bag of money. Next day Graham was found dead; the money was gone—obviously the thieves had followed him and killed him. Certainly it happened that way. What else could account for it?'

Mama was nodding her head in a pensive way, reviewing the gruesome tale, as I was myself. 'That sounds logical,' Mama said.

'That is the conclusion Bow Street came to, in any case,' Mrs Mailer said. I had my own opinion of Bow Street, but before I could voice it, she spoke on. 'I got my necklace back,

Lloyd's had to pay ten thousand pounds instead of twenty-five thousand guineas, and Graham got murdered. It is a sad story and best forgotten. I have never worn the necklace again. In fact, Lloyd's have become so very sniffy about insuring my jewelry that I no longer wear any of it. I have it all locked up in a bank vault and make do with these old gold chains. I've been frightened to death to put on anything valuable since the night I was robbed.'

'What? You never mean it was taken off yourself!' Mama gasped. 'I thought it must have been stolen from your house.'

'Devil a bit of it. It was ripped from my neck, on my own doorstep. I was returning from a party with a gentleman friend. Mr Thomson, a very good friend. Two Legs Thomson, folks call him.'

'Why do they call him that?' Esther asked.

'Because he has two legs, goose! His twin brother has only one. It saves calling poor Limpy "One Leg", you see.'

'Rather thoughtful, really. Mr Thomson and I had gotten out of the carriage. He was with me at the door saying good night when a very tall man appeared from behind the bushes. He reached down and wrenched the thing from my neck, leaving me with a dreadful bruise.' She rubbed her neck as though it still hurt two years later. 'He had on a mask. He darted off toward the back of the house. I was so distraught I clung to Mr Thomson for a moment, and by the time he could give chase the man was gone. Got away clean as a whistle, and no amount of hinting by the insurance agent ever proved I had a thing to do with it. I never saw the thief before in my life, or since. All I can say is that he was very tall and quite thin. Not an old man, to judge by the speed of his flight after he had stolen my necklace. It was a common thief. The few words he spoke were hardly intelligible, though Mr Thomson seemed to understand his jargon. Those thieves have a cant all their own. Many of the fashionable bucks are imitating them nowadays. Strange, is it not, how such disreputable persons can set a fashion? But young Sedgley actually had his front teeth filed down so he can whistle like the mail coach drivers. And they call us women vain and foolish!'

I remembered Mr Desmond using the same incomprehensible lingo that morning, and while the detail was in my mind I asked Mrs Mailer if she knew him, since he appeared to know a little something about me.

'Mr Desmond? No, I don't recall anyone by that name. But then one meets so many people.'

Mama blinked at the thought that she could have forgotten the name of an acquaintance. 'London is a shocking place,' she said. 'I always heard it was wicked, but I never knew how bad it was till we spent these few days here. People coming into your house, turning it upside down, stealing your jewels, murdering poor Graham.'

'What? Has someone broken into your house?' Mrs Mailer demanded.

We described the shambles that had first greeted us and our precaution of having new locks installed, and as we spoke a crafty look stole over her face. 'A wise move. He was after the money, certainly,' Mrs Mailer decreed.

'You said the thief came in and killed Graham and took the money,' Mama reminded her.

'That was our assumption at the time. It seems we were mistaken. Why would he keep coming back, unless to look for the money? Graham was so sly there was no outwitting him. He hid the money somewhere, and the thief didn't find it. It is in this house, Belle, and if you have your wits about you, you'll get busy and find it. A fortune!'

'Not my fortune. It would have to be returned to the insurance company.'

She looked at me as though I were a simpleton. I had not realized till then that she was as black-hearted as any inhabitant of Bridewell or Newgate. We stared at each other a long moment, each realizing with incredulity that the other was serious; then our eyes parted. 'Yes, of course,' she said, laughing nervously.

Over tea we talked about mutual friends in Bath, and after half an hour Mrs Mailer rose to leave. At the door she said, 'So you are determined to sell the house, are you, Belle?'

'Yes, my mind is made up.'

Esther stood behind me, hoping to cajole an invitation from Yootha before she left. I was coming to the conclusion that her friends would not be agreeable to us. She was too racy, too Londonized, her character too unsteady.

'It happens I know someone who is interested in a small spot like this. I'll bring him around tomorrow, shall I?' Mrs Mailer asked.

'By all means. There is no saying Mr Desmond will take the house.'

'What time does Desmond come?'

'At eleven.'

'Hmm. Ten is too early. I'll bring my friend at twelve. We must get together soon for dinner or a play. We'll decide tomorrow after I look over my calendar. I have an engagement this evening.'

'We're free any night!' Esther assured her.

'You'll have every rake and rattle in town camping on your doorstep once they get a look at you,' Mrs Mailer promised gaily.

'Not if I know anything. She's only seventeen!'

'Only seventeen! My dear, I had been married for over a year at the advanced age of seventeen. *Only* seventeen!' she repeated, and went laughing down the walk to her carriage.

While Mama and Esther discussed Yootha's pending invitation, I thought about her story of Graham's death—and, of course, about the possibility that we were sitting on ten thousand pounds. Before dinner, I searched the house from attic to cellar without finding the money. I found a ring of keys in the kitchen, and while I was in the attic unlocking those three trunks and discovering nothing but blankets stored in camphor, the lawyer sent over the parcel containing the clothing Graham had worn the night of his death. Mama put the bundle in the master bedroom, where it sat like a ghost, awaiting examination.

After dinner I planned to open the parcel but felt a pronounced reluctance to do so. I took the absurd idea that some new horror would be unleashed if I drew the string. Evening wasn't the time for it. I'd confront that last ghost of Graham in the bright light of morning.

We retired at ten-thirty that night, in spite of our lovely gaslight. I lay in bed reviewing the curious events and people of the day. Bow Street Runner and nosy neighbors, locksmith and Yootha Mailer, who thought I should steal the ten thousand guineas, if I could find it. And last I thought of the most intriguing of them all, Mr Desmond, who knew I was to have been married, who knew Papa was a

51

clergyman, who had casually mentioned the possibility of a bag of gold being in the attic. Actually, Yootha had said it was banknotes. Ten thousand pounds in gold would be too heavy for one man to carry, but 'gold' was a figurative way of saying 'money.'

Mr Desmond also spoke that jargon not used by decent, law-abiding citizens. Thieves' cant, Harrow called it. Where did these fashionable bucks learn thieves' cant but from thieves? And if Mr Desmond associated with thieves—but it was a long step to accuse him of being involved in Graham's death. He didn't have the face of a thief or murderer, but of a fashionable flirt. Still, I'd bear it in mind tomorrow when he came with his builder. One character Yootha mentioned whom I had not met yet also held interest for me. I was very eager to meet Graham's cousin, Eliot Sutton. He, at least, should be above any sort of suspicion. If he was to be a part of the social do Yootha would arrange to entertain us, I would accept. He might even provide a flirt for Esther—or for me.

CHAPTER FOUR

The next day was a busy one. With no servants to help us, we three women had to bring the house to order for showing to two groups of people. I couldn't say which pair took a closer look, Yootha and Two Legs Thomson or Mr Desmond and his builder. Among the four of them, there wasn't a nook or cranny of the building that escaped investigation. Mr Desmond arrived with his man at eleven sharp, like a good businessman. His builder, Mr Grant, was a small, dark person with a face like a gargoyle and a body all lean and wiggly, like a weasel. He carried the tools of his trade with him in a leather bag and spoke that strange cant language that Mr Desmond occasionally slipped into himself.

They started at the attic and worked their way down a floor at a time. You could hear them tapping at the floors and walls with a hammer, and when I passed once in the hall I saw Mr Grant loosening a baseboard in the master bedroom.

'Take care what you're about, sir!' I called sharply. 'You are only to examine, not to tear the place apart!'

Mr Desmond came smiling to the door. 'The base-boards are very loose. Grant is hammering a few nails in for you. You don't want mice scampering over your pillow while you sleep.'

'Mice!'

'I don't think the crack was big enough for rats,' he assured me.

'It will be by the time he's finished. He wasn't tightening the boards; he was loosening

53

them.' Even while I spoke, Grant stuck three nails between his teeth, another in the board, and began hammering up such a storm that I had to leave to save my ears.

No castle ever received such a thorough going-over as my doll house did from Grant and Mr Desmond. It became quite a joke once they got down to street level, where the family was in their way and vice versa. I was in the saloon writing a few instructions home for the servants who remained there when Mr Desmond started on that room. I could have moved, but I liked the fire. 'Don't let me prevent you from what you're doing,' I said to Grant.

'You've got a rum ken here, Miss,' Grant informed me. 'Nothing to fear but star glazers, maybe.'

'I beg your pardon.'

'Stubble it, Grant,' Mr Desmond said. Grant scowled and turned back to work.

I had a definite impression the men wished me elsewhere, but I felt that three quarters of an hour had been more than ample for their examination, and I sat on, watching Grant from the corner of my eye. Before long his employer took up a chair beside me to distract my attention. 'I have a few questions to ask, Miss Haley, with your permission,' he said, smiling politely.

'Certainly. Go ahead.'

While Grant groveled around the floor

pulling at quarter-round and wainscoting, Desmond posed a series of pointless questions I couldn't have answered if I'd built the house with my own two hands. What age was the building, what were the external measurements, was the paneling in the dining room oak or cherry or something else, was the paper in the master bedroom the original paper, and such things. I repeated that I did not know, could not really say, and finally I said bluntly that I knew no more about the house than he did himself.

'Probably a good deal less,' I added pointedly. 'I have been here less than forty-eight hours, and I have not hired a man to go down on his hands and knees and try every splinter. What are you looking for?'

'Termites, wood rot, poor construction— that sort of thing.'

'Have you found any of these flaws?'

'Nothing serious. Water has gotten in around the upper windows. There's a suspicious brown mark on the ceiling of the east bedchamber. The doors are all poorly hung, and the stairs squawk like an unoiled hinge.'

'I'm glad it's nothing serious!'

'Old houses always have imperfections,' he said leniently. 'Would you mind coming with me to the dining room? There's some irregularity in the paneling there.'

I peered around his shoulder to see what

55

Grant was up to. Using the sofa as concealment, he was sliding a screw-driver between the wooden panels. 'We'll have greater irregularities in the saloon if you don't call Mr Grant off.'

'Take it easy, Grant,' Mr Desmond ordered.

Grant looked over his shoulder and said slyly, 'Aye, the mort's whiddled beef on you, lad.'

'What is he talking about?'

Mr Desmond took my elbow and hastened me across the hall to the dining room. 'Mr Grant's from Ireland. He speaks a strange sort of dialect, related to Gaelic, no doubt.'

'Or to thieves' cant, perhaps?'

He frowned at me, as though not understanding my jibe.

'Now about this paneling,' he said, gazing at it. The wood was imperfect to be sure, but no more so than any other paneled wall that's seen a few decades of use. 'This side of the room is darker than the other,' he pointed out, peering from one side of the room to the other.

The darker side doesn't receive light from the window,' I explained.

'Shall we just turn on the gaslight?'

'If you really think it's necessary.'

He did, and still he imagined one wall to be darker than the other. 'A different shade of stain was used, I expect. The difference is hardly startling,' I said. 'I hadn't noticed.'

56

'You haven't been using the dining room.'

'What makes you think so?'

The toast crumbs on the living room carpet,' he answered blandly.

'Our servants aren't here yet.'

'How awkward for you,' he said, oozing an inordinate amount of sympathy.

I peered back into the saloon. Grant had disappeared behind the sofa again. 'It isn't the servants we miss so much as the carriage, actually. We hadn't planned to stay long.'

'I will be very happy to deliver you anywhere you wish to go.

'That's kind of you, but I know you're very busy. We can always hire a hackney.'

Sympathy escalated to flirtation to distract me from Grant's racket across the hall. 'You rob me of the opportunity to know you better, ma'am.'

I gave him a meaningful stare and said, 'You already know me better than I know you, Mr Desmond. You know my father was a clergyman and that I was to have been married. Were you acquainted with Graham Sutton?'

His head came forward a moment, and he frowned, as though not hearing, or not understanding. 'With whom?'

'My late fiance, Graham Sutton.'

'I'm afraid I had not the honor, but I should like to have met him. I admire his taste.' The boldest pair of eyes in London roved admiringly over my face as he said this.

Aware of a warm flush creeping up my neck, I immediately pretended to misunderstand. 'Now, that's odd. You've done nothing but disparage his taste in homes since you've come here.'

'I think you knew it wasn't architecture we were discussing, ma'am. I plan to buy the house, and if I develop an interest in acquiring permanent rights to . . .'

It was a great relief when this piece of impertinence was interrupted by a resounding crash from the saloon. 'That wretched man is destroying my house!' I exclaimed, and dashed across the hall with Mr Desmond hard at my heels.

Mr Grant had taken the notion to detach a built-in cupboard from the wall. He had not quite succeeded in his aim but had managed to shake loose a pile of books from a shelf, which had caused the noise.

'Try to be more quiet, Grant,' Mr Desmond said severely.

'No need to ride rusty. Ain't I dirtying my finest duds for you?' Grant complained, but he picked up the books.

'About the furnishings, Miss Haley,' Mr Desmond said, and took my arm to leave the noisy saloon.

'With a few exceptions, they would be included in the price of six thousand.'

'And the wine in the cellar?'

My eyes narrowed at this question. He hadn't been to the cellar yet, nor had he gone there yesterday. How did he know the cellar was full of excellent wines?

'What makes you think there's any wine in the cellar?'

'Where else would it be?' he asked. 'Naturally I assumed a gentleman had put down a cellar.'

'Of course he did! The wine is not included,' I said, because I was angry at being made to look foolish.

'Wine travels poorly,' he cautioned playfully, haggling over it. 'Except from cellar to table, and thence to glass, if a gentleman is lucky.'

He seemed genuinely interested in buying the house, and to keep him in humor I offered a glass of sherry. Mr Desmond might know something about Graham's business, but if he was disappointed not to find a bag of money when he moved in, it was hardly my fault.

Over the wine, conversation turned from business to mere social chitchat. 'Are you an established resident of London, Mr Desmond?'

'We are a Devon family, but I've been in London for upwards of ten years and consider myself a Londoner.'

'You must give me some idea what sights are worth seeing. My young sister is eager to tour the town.'

'And are you, also being a young lady, not curious, Miss Haley?'

'I shall accompany her, of course.'

He regaled me with a list of attractions. Grant stuck his head in at the door and said he was going to 'cast his glimms over the dungeon,' after which he went to the cellar.

'How does it come you employ a man who doesn't speak English?' I asked politely.

'Grant's the best man at this sort of work. Every trade has its jargon.'

'If I am not mistaken, that particular jargon is neither Gaelic nor related to the building trade. It is thieves' cant.'

A look of surprise lit his face. 'How did you recognize it? Pattering flash at Bath Abbey these days, are they?'

'No, sir. I learned the rudiments of the language from Bow Street. I don't have to ask where you picked it up, and I do not appreciate your bringing a thief into my house. If Mr Grant has rushed a dozen bottles of wine out the cellar window, I shall expect you to stand buff for it.'

'I'll have to buy Jay a muzzle. I knew you'd be worried, so I didn't tell you the whole truth about Mr Grant. You need not worry. The spanks he charges, he doesn't have to nab nowadays.'

'And in *English* that would mean . . . ?'

'He's being well paid.' A shapely finger was waggled in front of me. 'A clergyman's

60

daughter should entertain more charitable thoughts than encumber your head, Miss Haley. I am endeavoring to reform Mr Grant and a few of his confrères. And here you thought I was in league with the scapegallows fraternity. Jay used to be on the ken lay—he robbed houses after he had carefully inspected them in his regular line of business. I caught him with his daddies in my safe one night. While I was delivering him to Bow Sheet he told me such a tale of woe that I decided to give him a chance to go straight. That was three years ago; he hasn't stolen anything since, to my knowledge.'

'You're quite a philanthropist,' I said doubtfully.

'I believe in practical benevolence—Jay provides good services for his keep. And along the way we've learned a little of each other's language.'

Grant soon joined us and said, 'There's rum quids in the hole, lad—'

'Much good it will do us. The wine don't come with the house. I'll meet you in the carriage, Jay.'

Grant ducked his head in what was meant to be a bow and left.

'Are you ready to make me a firm offer, sir?' I asked.

'I shall have to go over the report with Grant first. When may I return?'

'As soon as you make up your mind. I

should caution you that someone else is coming to look at the house today.'

A blaze of interest flashed in his dark eyes. 'Who is that?'

'I don't know the gentleman's name—he's a friend of a friend.'

'I see.'

Before he got out, Mrs Mailer and her friend were in. I first assumed the hostile looks they exchanged were due to their competition for my house. It was no such thing! They were acquainted, and to judge by their scowls, the acquaintance was not a happy one.

'Mrs Mailer, Mr Thomson,' Mr Desmond said, with a curt bow.

They nodded, more curtly still, but didn't speak.

As Mr Desmond left, Yootha and her friend charged into the saloon, their eyes wide with indignation.

'What is *he* doing here?' Mrs Mailer demanded.

'He's the man who is thinking of buying our house,' I explained.

'Mr Maitland? No such a thing!'

'His name is Mr Desmond,' I said, but already I knew I had been taken in.

'Desmond Maitland, that's who he is,' Yootha said.

Mama, looking all bewildered, asked, 'Do you know him well?'

'He is the agent who insured my necklace

and was so unpleasant about giving me my money when it was stolen,' Yootha announced.

'Do you mean to tell me the man is an insurance agent?' I gasped, and fell into a fit of giggles. He with his office at the Royal Exchange and his philanthropy, his fine carriage and jackets, and he was only an insurance agent. He couldn't buy a dog kennel, let alone a house. He probably owed every merchant in town to maintain his carriage and jackets.

'Not just any agent,' she continued. 'Mr Maitland is the man who put up the ten thousand pounds the night Graham was killed.'

We went into the saloon, and before we were seated Mrs Mailer presented her friend to us. It was Mr Two Legs Thomson, her latest flirt. Besides his two legs, he had two arms, two sharp gray eyes, one head, and so on, none of them exceptional. He was white-haired and wore the sort of red nose commonly associated with a liking for wine. He had a tendency to stoutness and was in every way a gentleman in his appearance and manner.

'Is it some sort of stunt Mr Desmond was playing off on us in coming here?' Mama demanded.

'Of course it was. Maitland no more plans to buy your house than I do,' Yootha exclaimed angrily. 'That is . . .'

'We know you aren't interested in buying it,'

I said, as she appeared to have become embarrassed at her speech. I looked with suspicious interest to decide by Two Legs's jacket if he could afford the house.

'He only came to see if he could find the money,' Mrs Mailer continued. She shook her head firmly at Two Legs as she spoke. 'It's here, I tell you. Right in this house, and Mr Maitland knows it. He is probably your burglar. He associates with the worst riffraff in town.'

'It will be a fine bonus for whoever buys the house. Perhaps Lloyd's will give the agent a reward when it is returned,' I said, to remind Yootha what was to be done with the money. 'Very likely that's why Mr Maitland was looking so hard.'

'He seemed such a nice young fellow, and he was full of deceit all the time,' Mama said, surprised into plain speaking. 'He told us he worked at the Royal Exchange.'

Two Legs drew his brows together and frowned at us. 'Eh? You have got it mixed up, ladies. Lloyd's offices *are* at the Royal Exchange. You sound as though Maitland were some demmed clerk. It is nothing of the sort. Each Lloyd's agent is an independent businessman—they buy a license for some enormous sum of money. They all finance their own losses. The ten thousand came out of Mr Maitland's pocket. They all belong to Lloyd's, but they work on their own, take their own risks, keep their own policy money, and pay their losses out of their own pockets.'

'He must be very rich!' Esther said bluntly.

'A regular nabob,' Two Legs assured her.

'Which is not to say he has the right to be searching Miss Haley's house for the money,' Yootha said firmly. 'That was an ordinary business loss, to be expected. That's why we pay them so much to buy our insurance.'

I began to perceive all the same that with such people as Yootha Mailer involved, Mr Maitland was wise to try to recover his money. My only resentment was that he hadn't been more straightforward about it. It was a slight against my character for him to feel the necessity of so much lying and conniving. I would gladly have given him permission to search to his heart's content and would tell him so next time we met—if we met again. I had a strong feeling it would take more than disclosure as a liar to keep Mr Maitland away.

'Did he find it?' Mr Thomson asked eagerly.

'No, he didn't, and he ransacked the house from top to bottom,' I assured them.

Assurance wasn't enough. Mr Thomson had to repeat the procedure for himself, using the pretext that he was just examining the house closely with an eye to buying it. I went with him and Yootha every step of the way. If anyone was going to find that money, it was going to be me. Graham's honor was not really at stake, but I wanted to perform this last

65

office for him. I noticed scratch marks on the locks of the trunks in the attic. Clearly the redoubtable Grant had pried them open and seen the blankets. The search convinced us all that there wasn't so much as a comb hidden in the house.

After the tour we returned to the saloon for sherry. Mr Thomson displayed not the slightest interest in offering for the house. All he wanted to talk about was the money. He and Yootha reiterated that the money must be here, or why did people keep coming to look for it? But in the end we all realized that the only one who knew was the man who had killed Graham; and as no one knew who that was, the rest was mere conjecture.

'The servants might be able to tell us something,' Mama thought.

'There were none here that night,' Yootha said. 'Meadows, his man of all work, had gone home, and his female servant didn't sleep in. Graham was alone. The police looked into all that.'

'It seems odd that Graham would let anyone in, when he must have suspected he might be followed. But then I daresay the fellow broke in,' Mama said, and shook her head sadly.

'There was no sign of forced entry, nor any windows broken. Nothing like that,' Yootha said.

'It could have been someone Graham knew, for that matter. Someone he had no reason to suspect,' Mr Thomson mentioned.

'Good gracious, Two Legs,' Yootha interjected, 'Graham hadn't told anyone. Pelty enjoined us to be very quiet about the whole matter. I told no one but you. And you were with me at a rout that night, so I know you had nothing to do with it,' she added, with a sharp look that petered out to a laugh.

'Mr Pelty?' I asked.

'The other fellow from Lloyd's who was Maitland's partner,' Mrs Mailer explained. 'It seems that when the value of an insured object is high, the agents will sometimes go snacks, and it was a Mr Pelty who shared the risk on my necklace with Maitland. Mr Pelty was quite agreeable to paying me the money; it was Maitland who arranged with some of his unsavory criminal friends to exchange part of the money for the jewel. Mr Maitland was called home suddenly to Devon that day, and so Pelty was left alone to arrange the matter. If it hadn't been for Pelty, we would never have known the details. Maitland was a regular oyster, and no polite one, either.'

Without thinking what I was saying, I heard myself reply, 'That's too bad.' Yootha gave me a quick frown, and I changed the subject. But what flitted through my mind was that if Mr Maitland had been in charge, perhaps Graham would still be alive. There was an alert intelligence about Maitland and a ruthless thoroughness that gave me respect for his competence. But then, his concern would not have been for Graham—just for the necklace.

Eventually our guests rose to leave. 'Come to dinner tonight,' Mrs Mailer offered. 'Your servants aren't here, and it will save you some bother. I'll send my carriage for you, and I'll invite a couple of gentlemen, too. That will please you, eh, ladies?' She smiled.

'You need look no further for one volunteer,' Two Legs announced, with a long scrutiny of me. Was it possible the old fool had me in his eye? I didn't know whether to laugh or turn him out the door.

Esther looked ready to burst into tears. 'We don't have any gowns!' she protested.

'Come as you are; we'll make it very informal,' Mrs Mailer insisted.

Mama clucked, but in the end she wasn't proof against Esther's enthusiasm and her own desire for a good home-cooked meal.

On the way out Mr Thomson remembered his alleged reason for having come on the call and said, 'I'll think about the house, Miss Haley, and let you know. I look forward to seeing you again.'

I nodded very coolly, to discourage him. I would have to be in touch with the newspapers about extending my advertisement. I hadn't had a bona fide client yet. Only nosy neighbors and self-serving insurance agents and Two Legs Thomson. But first I really had to do something about that parcel awaiting me on

Graham's bed.

I went upstairs and cut the string. On top of his jacket there was a little packet containing his diamond stud, his watch, and his keys. I took up the packet and looked at his black jacket. The sight of it proved too much for me. Not yet—I couldn't face it yet. I took the packet to my room and left the bundle on the bed. Perhaps I'd have Hotchkiss take care of it for me.

I put the diamond stud and the watch on my dresser and took the keys downstairs. It would be handy to have a spare key for the house. There seemed more keys than were necessary. Did the back door have a separate key? No, the brass key opened both the front and back doors, but there were two other keys. One for his office, likely, but what was the third? I'd take it to Yootha and see if Graham had had a key to her house. That was probably it.

After another picnic lunch, Esther cajoled Mama and me out for a walk. There was a raw, nasty wind in the air, nipping our noses and dashing us all to pieces. Mama was regretting that I had told Hotchkiss and Ettie to come on the coach, as it would have been convenient to have our carriage in the city. 'But then I daresay Hotchkiss couldn't handle so much traffic in any case. I never saw so much of it. Where are they all going, do you think?'

'To plays and parties and balls,' Esther sighed.

'Not in the afternoon, goose!' I teased.

'Perhaps one of Aunt Yootha's friends will ask you out,' Mama said, to cheer her.

I didn't like that sort of cheering. Any friend of Yootha Mailer's would be a poor escort for innocent Esther. 'Graham left me his carriage. I'll look into hiring job horses for the short time we're in the city,' I announced.

'You'd have to hire a groom, too,' Mama pointed out, but in a perfectly hopeful manner.

'I suppose I can afford it now.' How odd to be suddenly on the verge of being—well, not rich, precisely, but rich enough to hire a team and a groom, at least.

The wind caught my bonnet and pulled it right off my head. Esther and I went tearing down the street after it, skirts flapping, and had the pleasure of no fewer than three gentlemen of the first stare coming to our assistance.

'Wasn't that nice of them?' Esther said as they walked away, looking back at the pretty child. And she, artful girl, had pitched her voice loud enough for them to hear.

I didn't chide her but only gave her a knowing look. 'You're setting up to be a fine flirt, Esther!'

'It's only in fun,' she said. 'We'll never see them again, so there's no harm in it, and it was nice of them to help. Imagine, Belle, there must be hundreds of fine gentlemen like that in London, and you and I don't even have proper gowns.'

'Hotchkiss will soon be here.'

'Yes, but we still won't have the sort of gowns ladies in London wear.'

'Oh, yes, we shall!' I said forcefully. The decision came from nowhere. From the wind, perhaps, that had taken my bonnet and blown in three helpful gentlemen. If the wind was to be that generous, the least I could do was to provide us with suitable gowns. Even if we did not stay on, our London style would cause a great stir back home. I was assailed by the memory of Mr Maitland and his bold, laughing black eyes. Could I handle such a gentleman? London fauna were more dangerous than the tame fellows at Bath. But I was now able to take Bow Street Runners and Yootha's crew in my stride, and if Esther, at seventeen, was eager to tackle a beau, why shouldn't I? After all, Graham had loved me, so I couldn't be a total antidote.

'I don't suppose Mr Maitland will be there tonight,' Esther said suddenly.

'Mr Maitland! No, I should think not. Aunt Yootha has no opinion of him.'

'The one who gave you back your hat reminded me of him. Did you notice what a handsome smile he had? He winked at me, Belle. What should I do when a gentleman winks at me?'

'A lady is oblivious to uncivil behavior, Esther. And she does not encourage a flirt—at

71

least not till she's been formally introduced,' I added more leniently.

We burst into laughter at the same moment. Mama was invaded by the same silly spirit and laughed along with us. 'Oh, my, speak of the blind leading the blind. You giving Esther lessons in how to manage a gentleman, Belle. It is hard to know which of the pair of you is the greater green-head! And I no better myself,' she added truthfully. 'What is to become of us here in London alone?'

She meant without Papa, and though she tried to feign desperation, I suspected there was a bit of pleasurable excitement mingled with it. Mama was not much over forty. And for more than half of her life she'd been a clergyman's wife in dull, provincial Bath. I think she was enjoying this little trip as much as Esther. Maybe even as much as I was.

CHAPTER FIVE

We did the best we could with our appearances, but going to dine in an afternoon gown took the edge off the visit for me. Esther supplied all the enthusiasm Mama and I lacked. She chattered like a magpie as she darted from room to room, borrowing blue ribbons from me, a small pearl necklace from Mama, and by the time Yootha's carriage arrived we were as nervous as a coop of setting hens.

Good as her word, Mrs Mailer supplied us all with escorts, even Mama. The Mr Stone in question was a friend and coeval of Two Legs Thomson. Like Thomson, he was red of nose and stout of stomach. Unlike him, he had no white hair, nor any other color either, except for a bit of soft gray fringe around the edge of his skull that gave his head the look of a billiard ball sitting in a roll of dust.

Her introductions led me to fear that the unfortunate-looking stump of a man named Duke was destined for me. He was Ralph Duke, not the Duke *of* anything. His height was even less than my own, and I am not overly tall for a lady. After he had sized me up, his face took on the expression of a peevish mullet. What he lacked in height he made up in weight. It was really astonishing that a man of twenty-five or so years should have acquired such an unsightly bulk around his middle section. His face, other than the expression, was not bad, though more childish than I like: blue eyes, a turned-up nose, cheeks suspiciously smooth.

He opened his lips to speak, but no words came out. His eyes had discovered Esther. There was a churning sound in his throat, as if a pepper mill had been put into action, and finally he found his voice. 'Good evening. Er, good day—er, good evening, Miss Haley,' he said, switching the time of day as he considered the hour and my toilette.

I curtsied and said, 'Good evening, Mr Duke.'

'Too bad about your house. Being ransacked and all, I mean to say.' His eyes wavered away to Esther.

'Yes, a pity.'

'Sorry about Graham, too, while I am about it. I knew him.'

This was his first interesting utterance. I attempted to follow it up, but the acquaintance appeared to be slight, and through Yootha's friend Mr Stone, who was Duke's uncle. 'We said good day a few times,' he informed me. 'Once on Bond Street, and once somewhere else. Here, I think it was.'

I concluded Yootha had scraped the barrel to find two young gentlemen for Esther and me. But all this was really at the back of my mind. Through an archway I had spotted a more interesting gentleman altogether, and I was waiting for him to join us. I could see by his profile he was too suave and too mature for one of Esther's tender years, which was bound to have her flirting her head off.

Then he turned toward us, and my heart nearly stopped beating. For a moment I had the mind-boggling idea I was looking at Graham, suddenly returned to earth. He stood at some distance from me, framed in a doorway, like a painting. Light shone all around him, from the chandeliers overhead and from side lamps. The man was the general size and shape of Graham, but it was at his head that I stared. He had the same high, noble brow as my fiance, with the hair growing in a pronounced peak in front. Our eyes met, and we stood gazing mutely at each other, not smiling, not even moving. Around me the slightly nervous talk of introductions whirled, but I was lifted above it all. My feet took command of the situation and wafted me toward the apparition in the next room.

I was aware of a bobbing motion at my shoulder and heard Mr Duke say, 'Eliot's the one who can tell you all about Graham. Daresay that's what you would like.'

Of course the man was Graham's cousin, Eliot Sutton, but the resemblance was uncanny enough to have startled me. As I drew closer to him I could see the differences clearly. I had to admit Eliot was more handsome. His features were more clearly defined, his nose stronger, his jaw more square; the hair on his head grew even more beautifully, but it was the same rich chestnut color. Mr Sutton didn't smile; he wore the solemn expression the occasion called for.

Mr Duke attempted to perform the introduction. 'Eliot, this is Miss Haley— Graham's . . . the lady who was engaged . . . that is to say . . . Miss Haley, this is Eliot Sutton.'

'How do you do,' I said, and offered him my hand while my eyes continued to drink in this reincarnation of Graham. He held my fingers tightly in a warm grasp for a little longer than the normal handshake.

'Miss Haley, I'm delighted to make your acquaintance. I meant to call on you as soon as you were settled in. I feel I know you already, as I heard my cousin speak of you so many times. I hope we shall be very good friends.' Even his voice had the rich, sincere timbre of Graham's. Then he noticed that he was still holding my hand, and he released it hastily.

'I hope so indeed.'

Mr Sutton led me to a sofa, and we sat a little apart from the others, with Duke crouched beside us, listening. To prevent Mr Sutton from taking the idea I was a moonling, I tried to explain myself. 'I'm sorry if I stared at you. It's just that there is such an astonishing resemblance between you and Graham. It startled me.'

'Dead ringers!' Duke muttered.

'We were often mistaken one for the other by slight acquaintances,' Mr Sutton agreed, 'but as we become better friends, you will learn I can't half live up to my cousin's virtue.'

He said all the proper and thoughtful things about Graham, expressed his condolences on my loss, and then wrapped that sad topic up in polite ribbons. 'But life goes on, Miss Haley.'

'It does, you know,' Duke confirmed.

'Now it is time for you to think of the future,' Sutton continued. 'I insist you treat this visit to London as the holiday it ought to be and enjoy yourself, as Graham would want you to. I intend to see you follow my orders. That I share with Graham—a dictator!' He smiled. No dictator had such an enchanting smile.

'Oh, I am enjoying it, except for certain minor irritations,' I assured him.

'Aunt Yootha told me about your difficulties. Please feel free to call on me if there is any problem that requires a man's intervention. I am unhappy you ladies have no man about the place. If Maitland returns to pester you, let me know and I'll speak to him.'

'As to that, I'm the one ought to speak to Des,' Duke interrupted. 'Thing is—a bit of a pal of mine. I'll tip him the clue. Not like Des to be so rag-mannered.'

I was surprised to hear Duke and Maitland were friends, for they were of such very different types. 'I doubt we'll see him again, since he's been exposed, but really I hardly blame him for trying to recover his money. It is only natural.'

'The way he went about it is not natural, but very havy cavy,' Mr Sutton insisted. 'Why did he not write you a letter and explain himself?'

'That occurred to me, too,' I said. Duke scratched his ear, but he had no excuse to offer on his friend's behalf. 'It is odd the way he

77

went about his business, but he knows now the money is not at Elm Street. I don't think he'll bother us again.'

Mr Sutton nodded thoughtfully. 'Don't let an unfortunate beginning put you off our city. London's not really such a bad place, you know. And have there been any other troubles? The lawyer has discharged all his duties, I trust? Turned over Graham's carriage and personal effects?'

'Not the carriage—though he gave me a letter telling me its location and directing the stable to turn it over to me when I want it. I am thinking of hiring job horses for the duration of our visit.'

'Now there is one way I might be able to help you! Let me hire the team for you. A lady can't go down to Tattersall's. If you want to give me the solicitor's letter, I'll collect the carriage as well. You'll need a place to stable the rig and horses.'

I smiled gratefully at his kindness. 'We could use some help in such matters. I expect I'll put the carriage up for sale when we leave.'

'It was a dandy landau Graham had. It won't be any problem finding a buyer,' Mr Sutton said. 'I expect you'll want to dispose of other personal effects as well. I'll tell you what, Miss Haley, why don't you let me take charge of all that? You won't want to have to sort through his shirts and boots—it would be too painful for you.'

78

'I was going to have Hotchkiss, our servant, do it, but you would have a better idea how to dispose of Graham's things. I want to give it all to charity.'

'That's what Graham would want.'

Duke leaned forward and intruded upon our talk again. 'I didn't hear any details about your house being torn apart, and about Des having the gall to let on he wanted to buy it. He is up to anything.'

'Why don't you speak to Miss Esther, Duke?' Sutton suggested in a patient way.

'Eh? Thought *you* was supposed to . . . That is . . . By Jove, she's a taking little thing, ain't she?'

'Very pretty,' Mr Sutton agreed. He shook his head and rolled his eyes ceilingward as Duke wobbled up and sauntered across the floor to make a bow to Esther.

'He is really the best of good fellows,' he assured me. 'A bit of a trial to his friends, but we all tolerate his idiosyncracies. And he is extremely eligible, too.'

'But is he of sound character? Esther is a simple Bath miss. I don't want her meeting just anyone.'

'Despite his being a friend of Maitland, Duke is unexceptionable,' he assured me.

'And is Mr Maitland less so?'

Mr Sutton considered the question gravely. He was like Graham—he wouldn't blacken a man's character unjustly. When he spoke, his words were tempered. 'I don't think he is a gentleman Graham would want you to know. I don't mean to imply he is a scoundrel, but he is a city buck, and young ladies from Bath might find him unmanageable.'

Esther had been casting covetous eyes on Mr Sutton and didn't waste any time in joining us. Duke got up and followed like a puppy at her heels. 'Did you remember to ask Aunt Yootha about the key, Belle?'

'Mrs Mailer, Esther!' I reminded her. 'No, not yet.'

'What key?' Duke asked.

I explained about the key in Graham's parcel, and Mr Sutton went to ask Yootha about it.

She came forward to have a look. 'No, it's not for my house. Graham had no reason to have a key, but try it anyway if you like.'

Her saying he didn't have a key was good enough for me. I was surprised when Mr Sutton went and tried it in the lock. What did he mean by doing such a thing? It was almost a hint that Graham had gotten a key without permission. Esther and Duke went with him, and I did likewise. Of course the key didn't fit Yootha's lock—how could it? He unthinkingly slid the key into his own pocket when he was finished.

'I'll take the key, Mr Sutton,' I said, and held out my hand for it.

'Oh, forgive me! I wasn't thinking what I

was about,' he said, and gave it to me.

As we returned to the saloon, he explained why he had wanted to check the key. 'The thing is, I had a key to Aunt Yootha's house a few years ago and lost it. I thought Graham might have found it. It was similar to that brass key. I used to keep an eye on things here for my aunt while she was in Bath.'

In the saloon I noticed from the corner of my eye that Mama and Mr Stone were engrossed in a discussion of Bath. Mr Stone was a regular visitor there, to take the waters. Mama was playfully chastising him for his lack of familiarity with the abbey.

'Next visit, you shall take me,' he said, and she blushed like a blue cow. Mama, imagine!

'Your Mama is churchy, I see,' Duke said to Esther.

'We are all churchy, sir,' she informed him. 'My father was a clergyman.'

'I went to church once,' he said solemnly. 'There were candles and singing. It was monstrously moving.'

'But it did not move you to return, eh, Duke?' Eliot roasted.

'I daresay I'll have another go at it. Bound to—marriage, funeral.'

Yootha served us a very fine dinner, and conversation was lively throughout. Despite the fact that Two Legs Thomson sat beside me, he didn't find an occasion to mention buying my house, but he did flirt outrageously.

'Have you thought at all of replacing young Sutton in your affections, Miss Haley?' he asked archly.

I bristled at his bad taste and said, 'No.'

'There's a deal of young prettiness going to waste, then.' He winked.

Across the table, I watched Duke watching Esther. He didn't eat two bites, and the meal was very fine, too. If he could pass a few more meals in this abstaining fashion, it would do his figure a world of good. But Esther didn't honor him with any flirtation. She was too busy batting her lashes at Eliot, and I think she received a little something in the way of encouragement, too, though he was properly attentive to me.

After dinner, the older members retired to a parlor for a few hands of cards, leaving the younger population alone. It was as good as a comedy to watch Esther try her burgeoning charms on Eliot and Duke try his more determined ones on her.

'My uncle Gerald is a bishop,' he told her. 'Perhaps he could give your papa a leg up the ecclesiastical ladder.'

'I don't think so. My father is dead, Mr Duke.'

'Ah, sorry about that. It ain't a bishop he needs, then, but an angel. No angels in my family. By Jove, you could have a word with those in charge above, Miss Esther.'

A shot from my eyes stopped him like a

bullet, and he sat rubbing his ear. Later there was more leaden-tongued eloquence from him, and before we left it was agreed that the gentlemen would call on us the next day.

'We cannot go out and leave Mama alone. We must either stay in, or all five of us go out together,' I insisted.

Eliot incurred more favor by coming up with a clever solution. 'Quite right, we cannot trust this pair of frisky puppies alone,' he said, honoring me with a special smile. 'We shall have your mama ride bobbin with them. Old-timers like you and me, on the other hand, Miss Haley, can be trusted to visit the Tower of London and St Paul's without falling into vice. We shall take two carriages and all meet there for the tours.'

'But you must have seen those attractions a dozen times. It will be boring for you,' I pointed out.

'I have not seen them with you,' he parried.

Duke looked much impressed with this piece of gallantry and tried to emulate it with Esther. 'You and I have never seen them together either, Miss Esther,' he said. 'In fact, I've never seen them with Mrs Haley either, though I must have seen them two dozen times with visiting aunts and cousins. I daresay the dome at St Paul's won't look much different, and the old hippo at the Tower will look as much like Lord Liverpool as ever, but if you've a mind to see them, I'll gladly pass up my afternoon at Jackson's Parlor and take you and your mother to look at old buildings instead.'

Esther considered this outing and found it better than staying at home. 'Very well, but we cannot go till afternoon. You promised me a new gown, Belle,' she reminded me. 'We shall choose our materials in the morning.' Then she turned her bewitching gaze on Mr Sutton and asked, 'What kind of gown would be proper for the theater, Mr Sutton? We plan to attend the comedy at the Haymarket—would it be possible for us to go without a male escort?'

'My aunt can better advise you on gowns,' Sutton told her, 'and as to a male escort—why do you speak of going unescorted, when I have given your sister firm instructions I am to be her cicisbeo during her visit?'

'Me, too,' Duke spoke up swiftly. 'I mean yours, Miss Esther. Very happy to be of use to you. I shouldn't mind seeing that tired old comedy again, I promise you. I have never seen it with you, in any case. About the gown,' he added, his voice wafting off as he gazed at her, 'blue. Sky blue, like your eyes.'

Esther primped her curls, waiting for the inevitable likening of them to gold, but the compliment didn't come. 'And bring a stout shawl,' Duke said instead. 'It's colder than Hades at the Haymarket.'

'I should hope so!' Mr Sutton laughed.

Duke gave him a heavy frown and added,

84

'Cold as ice is what it is. Miss Makepiece caught a chill when I took her there last week and blamed it on me.'

When conversation flagged, Mr Sutton suggested a little music. I play only indifferently, but Esther plays not at all, so it was for me to tackle the piano while he accompanied me in a rich baritone and Duke tapped out a counterpoint with his toes. We sang 'Tu Mi Chamas.' I selected it as it was one I was familiar with. Graham had often sung it for us at Bath while I played. If I closed my eyes, I could be back there . . .

The music brought the oldsters in to join us. We performed a few more numbers, and it was time to go home. We had four offers of a drive from the four gentlemen. It was Mr Stone who carried the day, much to my disappointment. But there was tomorrow to look forward to—a day filled with unusual pleasures. And when we entered our saloon there were enough embers that it was possible to build up the fire and warm milk for cocoa.

We discussed our evening and were all pleased with it. 'What did you think of Mr Stone?' I asked Mama.

'Poor Mr Stone, he is not at all well,' she said, shaking her head and happily taking on his troubles. 'The gout, you know. He drinks a little more wine than he should. I wonder if your papa would mind my playing cards for money. Dear me, and I fear I lost nearly a shilling, Belle. Mr Stone is such a clever hand with cards.'

Esther and I outlined the afternoon we had arranged and discovered to our astonishment that Mama had made plans of her own. 'Mr Stone is taking me for a drive,' she said, and giggled like a schoolgirl. I thought you would be here to stay with Esther, Belle. I had no idea Mr Sutton would ask you out.'

'Mr Stone—that old soaker! I wouldn't be seen dead in a ditch with him if I were you. It's no great matter. Esther and I will go together with Mr Sutton and Mr Duke.'

Esther was very happy with this arrangement. I was less happy, and quite unhappy that Mama was showing such signs of giddiness over Mr Stone. I was sure she would ask Esther and Mr Duke to join her, but she made no such offer.

'I begin to think it is you who need a chaperon, Mama!' I said in jest.

'At my age? Why, Belle, you cannot think it is romance! We are only going for a drive, and Charles mentioned stopping off to visit his daughter.'

'Charles, is it?'

'He asked me to call him Charles, but I did not ask him to call me Bridget.'

'Who is this Charles Stone, anyway?' I demanded. I heard echoes of Papa's stern tone and noticed that Mama assumed the mousish look she had worn whenever Papa was angry. I regretted it as soon as I had spoken.

'He's a very fine gentleman, Belle. He used to be an MP for some place in Wiltshire. Quite unexceptionable, and besides, I am only going for a drive with him.'

'Oh, Belle, you're as bad as Papa!' Esther chided.

'Your papa was not bad!' Mama said, and burst into tears.

That was the conclusion to our evening out. Such unusual social activity had left us all on edge. The tyrant relented and said more calmly that we must all be a little careful with London gentlemen.

'You weren't so careful with Eliot Sutton,' Esther reminded me.

'That's different. He's Graham's cousin,' I defended.

We soon went up to our beds. Memories of the evening floated through my mind as I lay trying to sleep. I thought of the little brass key and wondered whose door it opened. It niggled at my mind, but it didn't prevent me from enjoying my memories. Mostly I thought of Eliot Sutton, who was so very much like Graham. Was it possible he and I . . . But it was early yet for that.

CHAPTER SIX

We had just finished breakfast and were putting on pelisses and bonnets for our shopping spree when there was a knock at the front door. 'Maybe it's someone to see the house!' I exclaimed, and rushed to admit the caller.

I stood blinking at Mr Maitland, accompanied by Mr Duke, and a very odd pair they made, the one so tall and gallant, the other so stumpy and rumpled.

'As you see, it's me again, Miss Haley,' Mr Duke said, and stepped in uninvited.

'We are just going out,' I objected. Mr Maitland had enough manners to stay on the doorstep, but in the end I nodded him into the hall, as Mr Duke was already in the saloon, babbling some inanity to Esther.

'Jolly fine day, only as cold as bedamned, and a miserable gray sky,' I heard him say.

'At least it's not raining—or snowing,' Mama replied.

'We've come at an inconvenient time. We'll return later,' Mr Maitland said.

I was very curious to learn why he was here at all, and I gave some indication of this. 'I must talk to you,' was all he said, but he said it rather imperatively.

'There are a few things I'd like to say to you

as well,' I shot back swiftly.

He cast a disarmingly intimate smile at me. 'I wager there are. Who could blame you? But I want a chance to explain my farouche behavior.'

'As you can see, we were just leaving. I can't disappoint Esther and Mama.'

I soon deduced that Mr Duke had been brought along for a purpose. While Mr Maitland stood in the hallway, Esther came out wearing her bonnet. 'Mr Duke has offered to drive me and Mama to Bond Street, Belle, while Mr Maitland drives out with you to discuss the house. We are all to meet back here at noon, and you'll have to give us some money for the material.'

'What an excellent idea!' Mr Maitland exclaimed. He tried to pretend the notion had come from Duke, but I knew whose conniving mind was responsible.

'You'd best give me the spare house key as well, Belle,' Mama said, 'the one you found in Graham's parcel—in case we get home first.'

I went to get the key, and she came after me. 'Don't bring Maitland into the house if I am not home yet,' she cautioned. 'What do you suppose he can have to say for himself?'

'I shall soon find out.'

'You don't mind going with him?' she asked doubtfully.

'Of course not. He isn't a villain, after all.' Excitement was my prime emotion—

excitement and determination to call him to account.

Mr Duke's carriage was every bit as fine as Maitland's. A very handsome pair of black carriages was soon bolting down Elm Street. Inside Mr Maitland's there was a long silence till we reached Bond Street. I was collecting my thoughts and deciding how harsh I should be with him. Thus far I had only practiced my tyranny on such helpless victims as Mama and Esther.

Before I spoke, he entered into an apology that did much to disarm me. 'You'll be thinking London is even worse than you imagined, Miss Haley. I am sorry to bring Duke down on your head, but I was afraid if I came alone you'd set the dogs on me. I acted unwisely in trying to hide my true business from you. Duke tells me the term "havy cavy" was being bandied about last night with regard to my charade. If I had had any idea how agreeable you are, I would have approached you openly in the first place and explained my business. Once I had ensnared myself in that tall tale, I could find no graceful way out. The fact is, people have the idea that robbing an insurance company is like robbing the government—it's their constitutional right. But in this case, it is my partner and I who are each out five thousand pounds, and naturally we had to make some effort to get our money back.'

I thought of Two Legs and Yootha and had to admit Mr Maitland had not behaved so very badly. He had had no idea of my character; plenty of people would have tried to diddle him out of his money. 'Of course you had, but really, Mr Maitland, to get my hopes up that you meant to buy my house!'

He looked pleasantly surprised at the mildness of my attack. 'The oddest thing of all is that I *do* want to buy it—or, at least, I have an aunt who has expressed interest. But, of course, that is not why I had Grant ripping up floorboards. I was looking for my money.'

'It's not there. Whoever killed Graham took it, as Bow Street thinks.'

'But then why was the house searched afterward?' he asked.

'I don't know. I only know the money is not there now. Whoever did the searching must have found it eventually.'

He examined me a moment with his dark, intelligent eyes. 'That's not what the local locks say.'

'The locks?'

'The fencers, the men who deal in stolen goods in London. In my line of work I have to maintain close contact with them. Stolen goods usually turn up there, and it's cheaper to redeem them than to repay the whole insurance premium. Of course, it's reprehensible to have to dole out money to thieves, but what's our alternative? At any

91

rate, the word among the locks is that the money was never recovered. Jay Grant, my friend who frisked your ken, is in touch with the criminal element.'

'What about your partner, the Mr Pelty who actually performed the transaction? Is it possible *he* . . .'

Mr Maitland shook his head. 'No, he's above reproach. Pelty is almost too honest. Certainly he was too naive at the time to have engineered anything of the sort. I'm sorry he ever told Mrs Mailer about the transaction, but she was hounding the daylights out of us, and to keep her quiet he told her my plan. I don't want to offend you, but it struck me as odd that Mr Sutton ever involved himself in the business. It had nothing to do with him.'

'He was too honest, too, Mr Maitland. Any dishonesty was anathema to him. He was a solicitor, you know, and he hoped to become a judge eventually. He would have done the thing out of principle. Don't think he was criminally involved, for he was not. You don't know my fiancé if you can think that for one minute.'

He looked skeptical. 'I didn't know him; that's true. I have been judging him by his cousin, Eliot Sutton.'

I bristled in Eliot's defense. 'Surely you're not suggesting Eliot Sutton is a thief!' I objected.

'Not at all, but one has to wonder about a

gentleman with no income who doesn't work yet manages to live fairly high on the hog.'

'Does he not have any income?' I asked. Graham had a couple of thousand a year outside of his work. Yootha was also rich, and I had assumed Eliot was similarly endowed.

'I'm only going by gossip. He sold his little country place a few years ago to settle his debts. Perhaps he has enough to live and stave off his creditors till he marries some well-dowered lady.'

'You may be sure he has a competence,' I said firmly.

'In any case, Eliot Sutton has nothing to do with my affairs,' Mr Maitland continued in a voice that suggested he would be happy to change the topic. 'As you have surprised me so agreeably by being an honest and reasonable lady, I want to impose further on your kind nature and ask you to help me find my blunt.'

'How can I possibly help you, Mr Maitland? You and your bloodhound have been through the house with a fine-tooth comb.'

'I haven't looked through your fiancé's personal effects.'

'A parcel containing ten thousand in banknotes isn't sitting in a jacket pocket.'

'Not likely, but there might be some clue in a jacket pocket. That is the sort of place I would like your permission to look. Duke mentioned some key, for instance, that turned up last night and seemed to cause a deal of bother.'

'It didn't bother me! It was probably for something at his workplace.'

'He'd have an office key, of course. And there was just the one key unaccounted for, then?'

'No, there were two,' I admitted.

'Do you have them with you?'

'They're right here in my reticule. Why?'

'Let's run along to his office and see if either key fits it. You really should return the office key to whoever hired the place after Graham left.'

'I'm not sure where his office was.'

'It was on Jermyn Street, west of the Haymarket. A Mr Sinclair has the office now. I met him at the time of my investigations into Mr Sutton's affairs. Would you mind if we go there?'

I did mind, somehow, but it was such a reasonable request that I agreed. I didn't go in, though. I gave Mr Maitland the keys and I sat in the carriage looking at the modest, tidy little oaken doorway, now bearing the sign 'Sinclair and Humes, Solicitors.' Graham had spent five years of his life behind that wall—how strange that I knew nothing of his business there. Whole sections of my fiancé's life were unknown to me. I hardly knew him at all, really. Just as a tourist visiting Bath. In a moment Mr Maitland was back.

'One of the keys opens the door. Sinclair

never saw one like this,' he said, and deposited the single brass key in my hand. It was taking on a morbid fascination for me. It was more than a key to a door; it was a key to Graham, to some side of him that I didn't know.

The carriage returned westward to the more polite part of town, and we sat in silence a moment, thinking. 'You haven't given me your answer, Miss Haley,' he said a little later. 'Will you give me permission to look over Mr Sutton's private papers and effects? There might be some clue to what door that key unlocks and, more important to me, a clue as to where the money is.'

'Yes, you have the right to look.'

'Can we go now?' he asked eagerly.

'I'm afraid not. Mama is out, and this afternoon we are all going out. Tomorrow is the earliest...'

'Are you busy tonight?' he asked.

'No, we can't go out till we get some gowns. You may come early in the evening, if you'd like.'

His smile was approving—more than approving. It was a compliment. 'That's very kind of you. I want you to set your wits to work and think how I can repay you. I have already offered you the use of my carriage. Now I want to offer it in a way that will dilute your reluctance. This wretchedly rag-mannered man who has been annoying you—myself— don't necessarily come with the rig, you know.

Let me put it and a driver at your disposal while you are in London.'

I was touched by his thoughtfulness. 'We couldn't rob you of your carriage for a whole week, Mr Maitland.'

'Of course you could. Be *hard,* Miss Haley. You've seen how your polite virtue has been rewarded: by more incursions on your patience. You must learn to demand payment for your cooperation.'

'No, really—you are so busy.' Something in his smiling eyes led me on to roast him a little. 'Why, you'd be late for settling up day at Tatt's and for your dinner party with Lady Higgins if I took your carriage.'

'Not at all. I've already settled up at Tatt's, and I'll hitch a drive to Lady Higgins's rout with Duke. It's a pity you don't have your gowns, or you could all come with Duke and me.'

It pierced me like a knife that we had been such ninnies as to come to London without proper clothing. How dashing it would have been to attend a fashionable rout party, but it was not to be. 'Lady Higgins would be delighted to have three Bath provincials dumped on her, no doubt, but I'm afraid we must decline.'

'I know you must, this time, but I give you fair warning my sister is a hard patter. She'll be having more dos while you're here, and next time you won't have the excuse of no gowns.'

His eyes began an examination of my pelisse that made me terribly aware of its age and lack of fashion. 'You will, though, if you don't select your material. Your young sister and mama will have the jump on you. Shall we stop and select something for you now?'

I was thrown into a pelter at the thought of shopping with a strange gentleman. 'That's not at all necessary.'

'I am a famous judge of ladies' toilettes, Miss Haley. Liz—that's my sister—bores me all to Hinders with the latest styles. I can give you the names of the most dashing coiffeurs and milliners and modistes. You'll be top of the trees in no time.'

'No, really!' I protested weakly. I don't know why I bothered protesting at all. There was an irresistible force in Mr Maitland that didn't take no for an answer.

'If you prefer, we'll just drive along Bond Street and see if we can't find your family,' he said.

We alit when we reached the shopping area, and we strolled along the busy street, jostling elbows with the *ton*. Mr Maitland was sure enough of himself that he wasn't embarrassed to have an unfashionable lady hanging on his arm, gawking at the traffic and shop windows like a regular flat. He knew a great many people, at least to bow and nod to.

When we passed a drapery shop he said, 'This is where Liz buys her dress materials.

97

Perhaps we'll meet your mother in here.' As he spoke he held the door open for me to enter. I knew perfectly well I wouldn't find Mama in such an elegant place. She'd feel even more out of place than I did. But my timidity fell from me as I was confronted with whole walls of silks and sarsenets and Indian muslin.

'What color did you have in mind, Miss Haley?' His eyes flickered from my hair to my eyes, over my face, glancing off the blue pelisse I had on. 'What would go with that soft brown hair, just touched with gold, and topaz eyes? With winter coming on, you'll want a deep shade. Emerald green would suit you, or bronze. A bronze shot silk, perhaps . . . There's a lovely ell,' he said, pointing to the shelf.

As the shop was busy, I had some hope we'd get out without being served, but a clerk apparently knew Mr Maitland and came hastening forward.

'The lady would like to see that bolt, third from the top, if you please,' Mr Maitland said.

I stood blushing like a bride while the clerk scrambled up on a chair and brought down the bolt. Mr Maitland, who seemed to make himself at home everywhere, went behind the counter and took it from the man. 'While you're up there you might as well hand down the deep green one as well.'

Before I knew what was happening to me, he had my bonnet removed and a piece of the green silk draped over my shoulder. I knew the next step would be to lead me to a mirror to observe myself, and I dreaded it worse than a trip to the tooth drawer. I never wore such rich colors. The emerald would overpower my pale complexion, but there was no avoiding the trip to the mirror. The outing, or the discomfort of shopping with a gentleman of fashion, had put an unaccustomed wash of color on my cheeks and a flash in my eyes. I could nearly carry the color. I looked at Mr Maitland's reflection in the mirror, for he stood right beside me the whole time. I saw the indecision in his eyes.

'Would you like to try the bronze?' he suggested.

The clerk darted forward, removed the green, and draped the bronze across my chest. It was a taffeta that glinted in the sunlight and made me feel as if I were shining all over. Some reflection of the sheen was cast on my face. I looked almost pretty, and when I glanced uncertainly at Mr Maitland in the mirror I saw his lips lifted in approval.

'Top of the trees!' he smiled.

'Yes, this will be fine,' I said as calmly as I could, and removed the material. The woman standing in the mirror now in her plain blue serge coat was a different creature. She was only Miss Haley from Bath, not that other golden woman.

'What will you want with it?' Mr Maitland asked. 'Some blond lace, perhaps, or some ribbons?'

I chose both a length of lace to embellish the neckline and some narrow, dark brown velvet ribbons for my hair. It gave me an air of recklessness to be spending money in this fabulous shop amid all the ladies of fashion. I threw discretion to the winds and bought a pair of white kid gloves as well. The bill was inordinately high, but rather than bothering me, it made me feel good. Being irresponsible and foolish for once agreed with me. I felt like a different woman as we walked along the street, looking for Mama and Esther.

We didn't find them, and after a few blocks we reentered the carriage for a drive through Hyde Park. 'It will be livelier in the afternoon,' Mr Maitland mentioned, but it was already livelier than even the Pump Room at home, which is the most active corner of Bath in the morning. 'When you have the carriage you should drive down here around four in the afternoon and watch the ton disport themselves, if you are interested in such nonsense.'

'Of course we're interested!' I answered airily. 'We can do all the worthy things at home. While in London we plan to immerse ourselves in such abandoned dissipations as drives and theaters and routs.'

He reached out spontaneously and took hold of my fingers. 'Do you hear that, Miss Haley?'

I listened but heard only the turning of the carriage wheels and the sound of horses' hoofs. 'What do you mean?'

'That sighing sound . . .'

'Is it the carriage springs?'

'No, it's a sigh of relief. My carriage was afraid it would be taking a tour of all the churches and libraries.'

I laughed and pulled my fingers free. 'How absurd you are! And I have already told you, we don't plan to take your carriage.'

'You must.'

'Why must we?'

He cocked his head to one side and considered the matter a moment. 'Because I want you to, Miss Haley. How else am I to get on a first-name basis with you? You must admit it would sound odd for you to be telling your friends, "We borrowed Mr Maitland's carriage." They would wonder at your forwardness in accepting favors from a mere acquaintance. No, you must be able to say, "Des Maitland was kind enough to put his rig at our disposal." I know I should feel more comfortable saying, "Belle Haley is using my carriage" than "*Miss* Haley".'

'You have a novel way of looking at things, Mr Maitland.'

'Good, then it is settled, Belle. And now that you are being as agreeable as usual, I shall soon let you go home, as I know you have been wanting to do ever since we left the drapery store.'

'Oh, dear! My *gêne* was showing, was it? I admit I felt out of place there.'

'*Gêne?* No, not that. You looked delightfully confused and greedy, like a girl in a sweet shop. I only meant that when Liz buys a new bolt she can hardly wait to get home and start wrapping herself in it and wondering whether she shouldn't have chosen some other color or trim. Ah, and then the agonized bliss of choosing the pattern! Do you have a pattern book? I am privy to all ladies' necessities, you see.'

'You're stealing my very thoughts, sir!'

'Surely you don't object to such petty larceny? Er—you can delete the "petty." To imply your thoughts are anything but weighty must give offense.'

'Fashion is no petty matter, but Esther will bring a pattern book home.'

'Yes, but Esther will choose one that pleases *Esther.* I think Miss Haley would prefer something a little more dashing. I know Mr Maitland would.'

'Miss Haley's hanging a little past maturity on the family tree calls for stronger efforts at allurement, you mean?'

'Past maturity?' he asked, and laughed convincingly. 'The sulfur waters have preserved you uncommonly well, ma'am. I see no trail of the crow's foot yet, no corrosion of the brow. I'll send over some of Liz's books.'

These compliments were reassuring, and I was also happy to hear so many friendly references to his sister. A man who is on good terms with his family cannot be all bad. 'You are very close to your sister, I think.'

'She tolerates me, as I am a bachelor and useful for doing errands and filling an empty seat at dinner parties. Then, of course, it is always a married sister's prime avocation in life to see her bachelor brother shackled. I take it as a good sign she's happy in her own marriage. I wasn't sure she chose wisely.'

'Why? Is there something amiss with her husband?'

'Very much so. He has the misfortune to be perfect. I should think it would be very trying to live with perfection, wouldn't you?'

'No, I think it would be—perfect!' I felt that old, familiar, gnawing ache at losing Graham.

'That's what Liz says. Men must be different from women. Her husband is perfectly happy living with a pea-goose.'

It was an unusual outing. I had felt uncomfortable at the idea of spending a morning alone with Mr Maitland, but he was so very easy to get along with that I felt I had known him for years. It was a valuable quality he possessed, getting along equally well with clerks and criminals and ladies of all ages.

We descended from the carriage at the park and went for a walk. There was a cold wind blowing through the trees, but it felt good to get out and stretch our legs. Mr Maitland said he had to feed Lady Red, which caused a little confusion. 'She gets quite angry with me if I don't bring her a treat every morning,' he explained.

'Is she a beggar?' I asked in confusion.

'The most shameless beggar in the city. I'll introduce you to her.'

I wasn't at all sure I wished to add a beggar to my list of acquaintances. Already Mr Maitland had introduced me to a thief.

He had a bag of nuts in his pocket, and he began looking around the trees. Before long, a large red squirrel came and took the nuts from his fingers. I was formally presented to Lady Red. Other squirrels were content to retrieve the nuts as he tossed them about on the grass. He looked younger, less sophisticated, at this occupation. In fact, he looked like a boy.

A bold blue jay was making a wicked racket in the tree-top overhead. It was furious at being left out of the treat. When one nut landed a few yards beyond the others the blue jay swooped down and grabbed it up. 'Oh, Des, look!' I laughed. 'Now Lady Jay has joined your party.'

'Too bad for her. I have no sympathy with backward ladies,' he said, and crumpled up the empty bag. When he rejoined me he wore a triumphant smile. 'But I am happy she came, even if she wasn't invited. She surprised another backward lady into calling me Des,' he said, and put my hand on his arm to return to the carriage.

When we reached Elm Street I was astonished to learn it was twelve-thirty. Mr Maitland did not come in with me but carried my parcels to the door and arranged an hour to return that evening. Mama and Esther had already made sandwiches and were fast casting themselves into a pelter at my late return.

'We were afraid Mr Maitland had done something with you,' Mama chided.

'Oh, he did, Mama. He took me to meet a beggar in the park.' I laughed and told her the story.

'Next time I shall go with you and Mr Maitland,' Esther said 'Mr Duke is a dead bore. All he talked about were sermons and churches.'

'He seems a well-behaved lad,' Mama said approvingly.

'What did you buy?' Esther asked.

We examined each other's goods. Mr Duke had taken the ladies to the Pantheon Bazaar. Mama thought the merchandise there not quite so fine as mine. I didn't tell her the ghastly sum I had paid for my superior stuff, but I didn't regret it.

In the afternoon our other callers came to take us out. It was so strange to see Mama walk out the door on the arm of any gentleman except Papa. The feeling of change, of oddness, was mitigated by Eliot. There I felt dangerously at home, it was so much like being with Graham. We did the sorts of things Graham would have done, too. We went to see St Paul's Cathedral and Whitehall and St James's Palace and Park. Mr Duke kept us merry with his foolish chatter.

Inside St Paul's he stood at the back of the nave, holding Esther's arm. 'Now that is what I call a church,' he exclaimed. Earlier he had proclaimed St James's Palace what he would call a palace, and St James's Park what he would call a park. 'Shall we go down the aisle together?' he asked her.

Eliot smiled at me. 'Perhaps more is meant than meets the ear, as Milton said.'

Duke scowled fiercely. 'Eh? Let him say it to my face!'

We had a thoroughly enjoyable afternoon, and when we reached Elm Street, Mama and Mr Stone were just driving up, so we stood chatting a moment.

'How did you find your sister, Mr Stone?' I asked politely.

'We didn't go to her,' Mama confessed. 'We went instead to an art gallery—my, such pictures! Enough to make a lady blush.'

I gave Mr Stone my gimlet eye and he tried to dismiss me. 'Just letting down our hair a little.'

'What hair?' Duke mumbled. For once, I didn't rebuke him.

'When would you like me to come and clear

out Graham's things for you?' Eliot asked before leaving. 'Or shall I do it now, while I'm here?'

We kept country hours, and I knew Mama would be wanting her dinner almost immediately. 'Can you come tomorrow morning?' I suggested.

'As you don't plan to go out, why don't I come this evening?' he parried.

'We've been pounding the streets all day. I think Mama is tired.' There was no particular reason for keeping Mr Maitland's visit a secret, but I didn't tell him. He'd poker up and act offended. No, that was Graham! How odd. During the afternoon my mind had been busy turning Eliot into his cousin. Graham would have been stiff, but then Graham would have had a reason, as I had been his fiancée.

'I'll be here tomorrow at ten, then, if that suits you,' he said very agreeably.

'That will be fine.'

After he and Mr Duke left, I told Mama that Mr Maitland was coming that evening. 'Whatever for?' she asked, astonished.

I explained that he wanted to look for clues to his money, and she accepted it. Esther, the sly minx, cast a wise look at me from the corner of her eye but didn't say anything. All the same, she wore her new ribbons at dinner and borrowed the pearls again.

CHAPTER SEVEN

When Mr Maitland arrived at the door that evening we received two surprises. The first was that he was dressed in evening clothes, for of course he would be going on to his sister's rout party. He looked almost like a stranger in his elegant black jacket and sparkling linen cravat. The second surprise was that he came loaded down like a footman, carrying flowers for Mama, a box of bonbons for Esther, and a tin of salted nuts for me.

'My goodness, Mr Maitland, you didn't have to do that!' Mama exclaimed, but she was pleased with his thoughtfulness. She rushed off immediately to put her flowers in water.

Esther took her sweets and said, 'This is an unexpected compliment, sir. Are you implying I am not sweet enough?'

'Certainly not. I make reference to the cliche "sweets for the sweet".'

When I saw the label on my tin I added my thanks. 'I am honored, Mr Maitland. Now that I understand your reasoning, I don't have to inquire whether I am salty enough. This puts me in the elevated company of Lady Red, does it not?'

'You must know you've replaced the ladies Red and Jay in my esteem, Belle.' I gave him a heavy frown for using my name, but as only

Esther was present, he ignored it. We sat in the saloon for a few moments before beginning our work. Mama came back with the flowers in a vase and offered tea.

'Mr Maitland is on his way to a party, Mama,' I explained. 'I'm sure he would like to get away early, so he will want to get to work.'

He turned a mocking eye on me. 'You don't get rid of a barnacle that easily, milady. We require stiffer hacking. I'll accept your kind invitation to tea, ma'am,' he said, glancing at Mama, 'but your daughter wants to work first, I believe. Where would you suggest we begin?'

'Graham used his bedroom as an office, so that is the likeliest place,' I suggested.

Esther, eager for a little attention, asked Desmond, 'What do you hope to find?'

'Probably nothing, but I would like to look, on the off chance that I will learn something.'

Esther came up with us and sat on the bed, eating her bonbons and playing propriety while Mr Maitland rooted through desk drawers and I searched jacket pockets. I noticed him lift my packet of letters to Graham. He looked at the blue satin ribbon, looked at me, and put them back in the drawer. I went to the bedside table and opened the little drawer. There was a tin of headache powders, a book of essays, and a small ledger of Graham's personal finances.

I flipped the book open and glanced at the last page of entries, mostly pertaining to the purchase and furnishing of the house. Graham was a precise accountant. Several items were listed—the sofas and tables, the draperies and silver—but this would be of no help to Desmond. I turned back to the earlier pages, perusing the accounts and looking for any oddity. In January of the year he died there was a withdrawal of two hundred pounds, listed as K.N. As I looked down the months I saw regular withdrawals of smaller sums. Ten pounds, five pounds, twenty pounds. And in August, another two hundred pounds, all entered as K.N.

I cast my mind back, trying to remember what Graham had been doing at that time. January was the time I had first gone out with Graham to the Assembly Rooms in Bath. In August we had become engaged, but there had been no great expense in that. My ring had belonged to his mother, so even that hadn't been a purchase.

I closed the book and peered over my shoulder at Desmond. He looked up and noticed my secretive air. 'Did you find something?' he asked, and paced forward.

'Nothing interesting. It's personal.'

His hand reached for the book. Esther was watching, and rather than make a show in front of her, I let him take the book. He studied it, flipping back through a few pages. I knew when he discovered the K.N. entries. The pages stopped flipping, and a puzzled frown settled on his brow. He didn't ask to keep the book but returned it to the drawer and said, 'This is dry work. Do you think we could have a glass of wine?'

Esther was bored and hopped up to fetch it. Desmond waited till she was beyond hearing, then asked, 'Do you recognize the initials K.N.?'

'No, I don't. Do you think it refers to a person?'

'I assume it does. The initials aren't any recognized abbreviation.'

'Maybe Graham was supporting a needy relative. I'll ask Mrs Mailer and Eliot Sutton. It has nothing to do with your money, in any case. The last K.N. entry occurred in August, months before he was killed.'

'I noticed.' He looked around the room and saw the bundle of Graham's clothes on the bed. 'What's that?'

I told him quietly while I stared at the unhappy bundle. His hands came out and grasped mine in a warm grip. His voice was low-pitched, sympathetic. 'What a sorry business for you, poor Belle. Not at all the way you envisaged your first trip to London. Have you looked through that parcel?'

'Not yet. I couldn't . . .' My voice broke, but I blinked away the hot tears that wanted to ooze out. His fingers squeezed mine so hard it was painful. I pulled myself together and looked at the parcel. 'It must be done sooner or later. If there is anything of use to you, that's where it would be, isn't it? That's what he wore that night.'

Desmond lifted the jacket and shook it out before looking through the pockets. 'His watch and so on were in a separate packet with his keys,' I explained. 'Bow Street must have emptied them.'

'They would. Perhaps the waistcoat . . .'

He began a rapid search of it. There was only one item, a small address book in the pocket. I had often seen it, for Graham always carried it with him. Desmond flipped through it, one finger tracing the columns. His pointing finger stopped, and he gave me a quick, worried glance.

'What is it?' I demanded, and went to peer over his shoulder. I read, *K. Norman, 7 Fleury Lane, 2B.* 'That must be K.N.! Where's Fleury Lane?'

'It's a short street, near Long Acre, just west of St Martin's Lane,' he replied. 'Not a choice district.'

'Long Acre?'

'Near there, yes,' he said, and gazed at me thoughtfully.

'That's where the necklace was given over— where Graham hit the man and took the money. Desmond, do you think Graham might have dropped the bag of money off there? I mean, it's very close, and if he knew someone was following him . . . Oh, we must go and see

112

K. Norman.'

'I'll go. It's not an area to take a lady.'

'Fiddlesticks! What do I care for that? I'm going with you.'

'I admire your enthusiasm, but stop and think a minute. If K. Norman has had that money for two years and not seen fit to return it, well, that gives you some idea of his character. I couldn't possibly take you there. It would be unconscionable.'

'If K. Norman was a friend or pensioner of Graham's, then he was no criminal. I have a right to go. This involves me, too. You've already brought a common thief into my house, so never mind pretending you care a fig for propriety.'

He smiled his submission. 'You aren't going to forgive me for introducing Grant to you, are you, Belle? Very well, I'll take you, but under protest. Whoever and whatever K. Norman turns out to be, the acquaintance is on your own head.'

We heard Esther's footsteps on the stairs. Then, when she had made the trip, we both decided there was nothing further to be done upstairs and went down to join Mama.

We discussed our small find with her. 'K. Norman,' she said, and her spectacles glinted in the lamplight. 'Graham's mama was named Leader before marriage, so it cannot be kin on that side. He had a cousin Kenneth, but the last name was Sutton. K. Norman. It means

113

nothing to me.'

It was frustrating to think I knew so little of Graham's life. 'It's probably some client,' I decided.

'In that case, K. Norman would have been paying Mr Sutton, and not the reverse,' Desmond pointed out.

We had soon exhausted that topic and chatted about other things. 'Are you ladies settling in comfortably?' he asked.

'If you look very closely, you won't see any crumbs on the carpet tonight,' I assured him. 'Mama has learned how to get the stove going. She pours grease on top of the papers and logs.'

'Grease? That's dangerous, ma'am! You'll start a conflagration in the chimney. How much longer will you be without servants? I ask because I could spare you a fellow till yours arrive. I don't like to think of you here unprotected.'

'It's good for us,' I assured him. 'It teaches us independence. Why, I am thinking quite seriously of putting the door knocker on myself. I discovered a toolbox in the kitchen.'

'Let me do it for you,' Desmond offered.

Mama was quite shocked and protested, but before you could say one, two, three, he had gotten the screwdriver and attached our brass acorn to the door, only a little crooked.

'Are there any other odd jobs I can do while I'm here?'

'Oh, dear, no, so very kind,' Mama said She was beginning to be quite relaxed with him.

I reminded him that he was going to be late for his sister's rout. 'Good,' he said. 'This is really a business party to entertain her husband's associates and their families. These associates have mostly daughters—antidotes, every one of them. Why should I spend my whole evening with antidotes when I could be with the three prettiest newcomers in town? Newcomers have a special cachet, you must know. I've had not fewer than three gentlemen asking for your name, Belle, after seeing us on the strut on Bond Street this morning. I told them I didn't know,' he added facetiously. 'I didn't want to subject you to calls from dukes and barons.'

'Desmond!' Esther squealed. 'I should *adore* to meet a duke!'

'You've already met one, my child. Mr Duke speaks of nothing else but your blue eyes and golden hair. And something else—what was it? A nasty temper, I think it was.' But he said it so charmingly that she appeared to take it for a compliment.

'I mean a real duke.' Esther pouted. Mama clucked, but forgivingly.

Desmond tossed his shoulders and said, 'Duke's as real as they come. You can't wish him away. You've attached him, my girl, and don't think you won't be the envy of a round dozen older ladies who have him in their eyes.

Mr Duke may not be the prettiest blade in London, but he's well connected and a good bloke, too.'

'Good gracious, what should you want with a duke, Esther?' Mama asked. 'You wouldn't even know how to address him.'

'I hadn't planned to write him a letter!' she said.

'Nor to speak to him either, apparently,' I added.

It was well after ten when Desmond finally rose and took his leave. 'Even a barnacle must go eventually. I'll send my groom around in the morning for your orders,' he said.

'Not that again! I told you we don't want your carriage.'

'And I told you that you shall have it, want it or not. You aren't the only one blessed with stubbornness, Belle. Devon breeds a famous mule. Or do I mean an egregious ass?'

Whatever it was that was bred in Devon, the carriage was at the door at nine on the dot the next morning. I sent the groom off and determined that I would have Eliot hire us a team and get Graham's carriage from the stable very soon.

Eliot arrived at ten, as arranged. Mama came to the bedroom with us when I took Eliot up to pack Graham's belongings. Eliot had brought a trunk, which he and his groom hauled up the staircase. We soon had the packing down to a system. Mama and I folded the garments, and Eliot arranged them in the trunk.

'This is sorry work,' he said, running his fingers over a jacket of blue Bath cloth. 'I was with Graham when he was fitted by Weston for this jacket. We had an argument over the buttons. I still think they're too large, even if Weston did approve them.'

'What will you do with these things?' Mama asked. 'I mean, you can hardly offer used clothing to gentlemen, and they are really too fashionable for a workhouse, or for charity.'

'I know of a home for retired clerics—impoverished gentlemen. They are always happy to accept donations of this sort,' Eliot explained.

Mama liked that it was her special favorites, clerics, who were to receive the trunk. The job didn't take long. The shoes were the last to go in, wrapped in paper. Just before the lid was closed, Eliot frowned and looked at the empty closet. 'Where is the jacket Graham wore the night he was killed? I know he wasn't buried in it, for I made those arrangements myself. It was an older jacket and a striped waistcoat he had on that night.'

I looked to the bed and saw the parcel was missing. 'Did you see the bundle that was here, Mama?'

'I just set it there at the foot of the bed. Esther got the bedcovers all mussed last night, and I wanted to tidy them. Here it is.' She lifted the parcel to the bed, and we folded in the last of the clothing.'

'Well, that's done!' Mama exclaimed.

I wanted to show my appreciation to Eliot and decided to give him Graham's watch. I took it downstairs and, after he and the groom had taken the trunk out, I gave it to him.

'I know you already have a watch, Eliot, but I'd like you to have this. I'd never use it, and you were Graham's best friend as well as his cousin.'

His lips clenched in emotion, and for a horrible instant I thought a tear was quivering at the corner of his eye. I know his fingers trembled when he reached for the watch, and when he spoke his voice was unsteady. 'This means a great deal to me, Miss Haley. It is thoughtful of you.' He stood, just gazing at it, then drew a deep sigh and put it in his pocket.

'Will you have a glass of sherry before you go?' Mama offered.

'That would be lovely.'

I went to get the glasses and a plate of biscuits. When our glasses were filled, Eliot took the notion of proposing a toast. 'Shall we drink this bumper to Graham?' he suggested. I looked at his noble brow, so familiar to me through my fiance, at his sad, thoughtful eyes, and felt a lump rise up in my throat. I couldn't speak. The others said, 'To Graham,' and we all drank.

Eliot looked around the little saloon. There

was a wistful air about him. 'Every item in this room reminds me of him,' he said. 'This sofa, Miss Haley—how many we looked at before finding just the dusty shade of blue that "Belle" liked. He always spoke of you as Belle to me. I feel I ought to call you that myself.'

'I wish you would. We would have been connected if . . . Please call me Belle.'

'If you—you all—will call me Eliot,' he said, including Mama and Esther in the bargain.

We continued drinking, but it was a heavy atmosphere that sat with us, that ghost of the past. 'An excellent sherry, if I do say so myself. I put Graham on to this lot,' Eliot continued. 'How excited he was, setting up his cellar. What do you think of those wine racks, Belle? They came from a mansion in Grosvenor Square that was having its cellars redone. Graham had them under the windows, but I advised him to move them away from the draft, and he did so. They're more convenient for you, right at the bottom of the stairs.'

Too convenient. We've made some inroads into the collection already.'

'Why not? It will go with the house, and won't add much to the price, either. I don't expect you'll be carrying the wine off to Bath, at least?'

'Oh, no.'

'Have you had any more customers come to look at the house?'

'Not a soul,' Mama told him, but I

remembered Desmond had mentioned knowing someone who was interested.

As though the memory conjured up the man, Desmond came calling not two minutes later.

I went to answer the door and found him admiring his own handiwork—the acorn knocker. 'That's a fine job of carpentry,' he said, and gave it a tap. 'I'm here to lodge a complaint on behalf of my groom. He wants to know why you refused to drive out with him.'

The only way to handle such nonsense was to ignore it. 'Desmond, would you like to come in? Eliot is here to take away Graham's personal effects.'

'Perhaps it's not a good time for me to call, then. I just wanted to set an hour for our visit to K. Norman, if you're still interested.'

'Of course I am! But I have to get rid of Eliot first. Oh, dear! That sounds dreadful, and he's been so kind.' Yet despite his kindness and despite his resemblance to Graham, I was impatient to see the back of him so that I could go to visit K. Norman.

'When shall I come back? It really must be done in daylight. I refuse to take you there after dark. Damme, I wouldn't want to go myself.'

'He's leaving soon. Is two o'clock all right for you?'

'Fine. I'll see you at two.' He tipped his hat and strode off to his carriage.

I was shivering from the cold wind of the doorway when I rejoined the party. They all looked expectantly to see who was at the door. 'That was Mr Maitland,' I said briefly.

'What did he want?' Esther asked.

I did a little prevaricating. 'He just asked if he could perform any errands for us, as he knows we don't have a carriage.'

'He's been very kind to us,' Mama said, and went on to discuss his various chores.

Eliot looked unhappy when the name Maitland was mentioned. Before her story was done, a frown settled between his brows. 'I wouldn't have much to do with Maitland if I were you,' he said. 'He's only using you.'

I felt a hot rush of anger and hurried in to defend him. 'He's trying to recover his money, Eliot. There is nothing wrong in that.'

'*His* money? It was only half his. The other half belonged to Pelty. If you want my opinion, I think Maitland knows more than he lets on. He's always been thick with the criminal element. It would be a nice windfall for him if he could find the ten thousand and just keep quiet about it to his partner. He only paid five out of his own pocket.'

'He'd never do that, Eliot. He's a very nice fellow,' Mama assured him.

'I only know what I hear from Mrs Mailer. I know he was very reluctant to pay her when she had her necklace stolen. Some of his questions went beyond impertinence to an assault on her character. Graham certainly held him in contempt. I think that was half the reason he was so determined to recapture the money, so that Maitland could not bruit his unfounded suspicions around town. If Maitland had let Pelty pay up the twenty-five thousand as he had planned to do, Graham would be alive today. Can you of all people, Belle, really blame me for disliking him and being shocked that you are ready to receive him in this house?'

I felt quite weak with guilt after this attack. 'What has he found out so far? Anything of interest?' Eliot asked.

I was the only one who knew about K. Norman. I knew Mama wouldn't approve of my going to Long Acre, and I didn't intend to tell her, though I wished to discuss it with Eliot. 'No, nothing,' I said.

I wish you would keep me informed. I mean to watch that bird. In fact, I'm going to follow him now and see what he's up to.'

I went with him to the door. I had put the little address book in my skirt pocket and drew it out before he left. 'Eliot, do you happen to know who this K. Norman is that Graham has in his book?'

He took the book and examined it. 'K. Norman,' he said, shaking his head. 'No, I don't think so. Why do you ask?'

The thing is, he was paying K. Norman money,' I said, and went on to explain the amounts and times.

'January to August, you say. Yes, that brings it back. I remember it vaguely now. It was a client of Graham's. The man was badly beaten in a back alley one night. He had a leg broken and his face badly mauled. He recognized one of his assailants and swore out a complaint against him. Graham took the fellow to court and lost the case. He felt it was his own fault for having presented it badly, and he undertook to keep Norman himself till he was able to work again.'

'Why did he feel he was responsible? Surely he didn't pay all the clients whose cases he lost.'

'Of course not, but when he was representing Norman he had another, much larger case going, and he felt he hadn't given his best attention to Norman. The defense had a line of character witnesses for their man, and I don't know what all else. When Graham got a very large fee from the other client, he decided to share it with Mr Norman. Well, you know Graham—honest almost to a fault.'

'I see. I was wondering about it because of the address—close to Long Acre, where Graham retrieved the money that night. I thought he might just possibly have left the money there—if he knew he was being followed, you know.'

'I shouldn't think it likely, Belle. People like K. Norman are transients. I doubt very much if

123

he'd still be living in Fleury Lane two years later. And he'd be the last sort of person Graham would have entrusted that money to, but if you like, I'll look into it for you.'

'No, don't bother. I was just curious.' I felt there was no longer any use in going to Fleury Lane at all, but Mr Maitland had the address, and no doubt that bulldog would pursue it.

Eliot left, and I went back to Graham's room to tidy up and throw out the few oddments of worn garments not worth delivering to charity. The desk had to be cleaned out, too. I didn't want to leave such items as my letters to Graham for the purchaser of the house to read. I found a carton to hold the things and began sorting and discarding. I had to interrupt my work for lunch and to prepare myself for Mr Maitland's visit.

The visit no longer held any charm for me. Eliot had been quite right; I ought not to be on such easy terms with the man who was at least partially responsible for Graham's death. Oh, not legally responsible, but involved all the same. How had I let myself be conned into receiving him at home, achieving a first-name basis with the whole family? It was his easy manner, his quick smile, his well-practiced charm. Esther was victim to it as well. Even Mama was not entirely immune, but I was the one who had opened our doors to him after he had come with his deceitful story of wanting to buy the house. And he was still using that old stunt. Now it was a relative who was interested. He must have taken me for an idiot.

I had worked myself into a raw mood when the expected tap came at two on the dot.

CHAPTER EIGHT

'Your carriage awaits, madam,' Mr Maitland said with a graceful bow, and strode into the hall. On this occasion his only gift was a recent copy of *La Belle Assemblee*. He handed it to me with one page turned down. 'Liz suggested this one for you,' he said, flipping the magazine open to display a gown of daring cut that would be a nine-day wonder in Bath, if I ever found the courage to wear it there.

'Liz obviously has no idea of my style, or lack thereof,' I replied coolly.

'*Au contraire!* By now she is acquainted with all your idiosyncracies and is on nettles to meet you. I am charged with the chore of delivering the Haley family to her en masse for dinner as soon as the gowns are made up. She was determined to come to call, but I thought you would want to have your servants here before receiving company.'

'Yes, of course.'

I put on my bonnet and pelisse in the hall

while Desmond stepped into the saloon to greet the others. When I was dressed, I joined them. 'What will you do while I'm gone?' I asked Mama.

What caused that blush to stain her pallid cheeks? So wrapped up had I been in my own affairs, I hadn't noticed that she and Esther had made suspiciously grand toilettes for an afternoon at home.

'The modiste is coming to start our gowns, Belle,' Esther reminded me.

'I have your measurements,' Mama added, 'and if you want to choose a design, we can order yours at the same time.'

I held La *Belle Assemblee* in my hand. Did I dare to order that dashing ensemble Desmond suggested? I could always add another row of lace at the top after we got home, and meanwhile it would suit London very well. I flipped quickly through the pages and noticed that while the recommended pattern seemed daring to me, it was, in fact, more modest than most. 'This one, I think,' I said, and handed Mama the book, open at the page Desmond's sister had suggested. She stared from the picture to me, her eyes wide in astonishment. 'I'll add another row of lace around the bodice, of course,' I said, to gain acceptance.

'It's rather—citified,' was her mild complaint.

Desmond bit back a smile and came to my rescue. 'Yes, that's all the crack in London this season. We don't want our girl to be out of fashion, but I don't recommend young Esther tackle a decolletage for a few years. Which have you chosen, Mrs Haley?'

A discussion of her gown and of the menace of short sleeves in particular, diverted her from further recriminations against my choice. How did he know that Mama liked long sleeves and that the pattern could easily be altered to achieve this antiquity? But he was a regular con artist; he could manipulate everyone. He had managed to make me feel that any gown but the one he had recommended would look dowdy.

We left, and as we entered the carriage I was assailed by a very pleasant warmth from the hot bricks. He had a fur rug waiting as well. 'This is unaccustomed luxury for a provincial mouse,' I said.

'You must have noticed my efforts to citify you before now, Belle. I am still hopeful of keeping you here on Elm Street.'

'That brings to mind your customer for my house. You *did* say an aunt was interested, if memory serves?'

'I've given her Grunt's report. She thinks six thousand is steep and has ordered me to haggle you down to five, including the furniture. She'd go for five *sans* furnishings, however, and you could make another five hundred if you auctioned off the bits and pieces. We'll let her stew awhile, to turn her

127

tender.'

I didn't believe a word he said. He was too glib, too superficially obliging. Do you always play these stunts on your family, undermining their transactions?'

'I'm usually on the side of the under-mouse. Aunt Phoebe is well to grass.'

'Pray tell your aunt Miss Haley said six thousand, in a very firm voice. About this K. Norman business, Desmond . . .'

'I *do* wish you'd let me go alone. Fleury Lane isn't a proper neighborhood for a lady.'

'That's what I want to talk about. I've discussed it with Eliot Sutton and no longer feel it's necessary to go at all.' I explained who K. Norman was, and the unlikelihood that he would still be residing in Fleury Lane.

Mr Maitland wore a doubtful face. 'Are you telling me your fiancé supported his client for eight months out of his own pocket, to the tune of some five hundred pounds in all?'

'Yes, I am. You'd have to know Graham to understand. He was like that.'

'I see I've been using the wrong solicitor!'

'He earned a very large commission and paid Mr Norman out of that. Conscience money, really, as he felt it was partially his fault for losing the case.'

'I didn't see any sign of that large commission in his bank statement last night.'

My annoyance with him came to a quick boil. 'Why can't you believe Graham was good? Why are you so suspicious of everyone and everything? The whole world isn't like you, Mr Maitland!'

'It has been my experience that most of the world is a deal worse!' he snapped back.

'What can you expect when you choose to surround yourself with thieves and criminals? You should see if you can find a few decent friends.'

'Such paragons as Mrs Mailer and Mr Eliot Sutton, you mean?'

'They'd be an improvement over Mr Grant, at least.'

'Mr Grant is more a business associate than a friend.'

'You should be careful of your associates. A man is known by the company he keeps.'

'So is a woman!' he shot back angrily.

'Very true. In future I shall be more careful. And perhaps you'd be kind enough to have your carriage turned around now. I want to go home.'

His dark eyes snapped. 'This is your Bath Miss way of saying you don't want to see me again. Is that it? Not high enough in the instep for you? I prefer plain speaking, Belle. What's got your nerves in an uproar? Are you really petty enough to dislike me because my work involves a few disreputable types? Or is it my honesty in admitting to a doubt about Eliot Sutton's fairy tale? If you trusted Graham as much as you say, you wouldn't fly into the boughs at my doubts. You'd explain rationally why you think I'm wrong. You know in the bottom of your heart neither Graham Sutton nor any other solicitor ever forked over five hundred pounds to a client with no real reason. It isn't done. No man would do it.'

'Graham did it!' I said in what I hoped was a rational voice.

'Then he wasn't a man; he was a saint. Are you firmly enough convinced to let me put it to a test?'

'Go to Fleury Lane, you mean?'

'No, I was an idiot ever to agree to take you there. I mean let us go to Sinclair's office and get your fiancé's ledgers. They're there in a box at the back of the office. Sinclair didn't know what to do with them.'

'You should have told me!'

'I told him I'd pick them up today and deliver them to you for disposal.'

'Fine, let us go now.'

He drew the check string and directed his driver to Jermyn Street. I had to go in and sign for the box. It was a harrowing experience to encounter yet another ghost of Graham. He had rented the office furnished. There, at that desk where the skeletal man with spectacles worked at his papers, Graham had sat. He had spent years of his life in this dull, horrid little office. I had pictured him in some grander place, surrounded with beautiful things. This didn't look like my Graham. He loved luxury

130

and beauty.

I signed a paper and Desmond took the carton to the carriage. He directed his groom to drive around town while we went through the ledgers right there in the carriage. We knew what period of time we were looking for and found the entries from January to August with no trouble. I was surprised at the trivial nature of Graham's business. When he had spoken of his work he had mentioned briefs and precedents and settlements in a vague but impressive way. He didn't make more than ten guineas for most jobs, though he had a great many small real estate and will-related clients. There was no K. Norman listed at all, and no large fee that would have allowed him to pay K. Norman five hundred pounds. I stared in disbelief at the ledgers.

'There must be some mistake. These can't be all the records. What's in that book?'

He opened another ledger, and another, till we had scanned them all, going back five years. 'I don't understand. Eliot said . . . I think we should go to Fleury Lane after all.'

But he had become cold and withdrawn. 'You changed your mind about going; now I've changed mine about taking you. It was a bad idea.'

'Very well, I'll have Eliot take me.'

'No!' The word was a bark.

I didn't bother arguing. Mr Maitland had nothing to say about where I went, or with whom. 'Shall we go back to Elm Street now?'

He grimaced and wiped his chin with his fingers. 'Belle, we've got to talk. Quite frankly, I don't care a tinker's curse about the money. Well, maybe one little profanity, but there is something very weird going on here. I know you disapprove of my association with coves like Grant, but the fact of the matter is that there really is such a thing as honor among thieves. That ten thousand pounds didn't find its way to Stop Hole Abbey. That's the chief rendezvous of thieves. You might think that's no tragedy—that they didn't deserve it in the first place—but it's put a spanner in my business. I depend on the fencers to save money on settling claims, and since that time they've been very reluctant to deal with me. I've had to make some whopping payments. I first thought Mrs Mailer had arranged to have her bauble stolen, and I was very reluctant to pay up. She had had another large claim a year before, and that always makes us suspicious. *We* don't claim to be saints,' he added, taking a jibe at Graham.

'That's wise of you.'

'I found out, however, that Billie the Slash *did* nick her necklace, so I no longer suspect her—not in the necklace affair, though Morrison still feels she might have stolen her own ring the year before. It never turned up at Stop Hole Abbey. But the fact is that Bow Street claims the thieves followed Graham and

132

retrieved the loot. They didn't, so where is it? That's what intrigues me. If there's a new racket being used, it's crucial that I find out about it.'

'Do so by all means, but it has nothing to do with me. I would still like to go home.'

'Where else can I turn but to you? There has to be some clue, something we're overlooking. You have his house, his private papers and effects.'

'You've been through them all. I can't help you. I wasn't here at the time. I'm afraid you've wasted your time and your talents, Mr Maitland, to say nothing of your flowers and treats.'

A slow, disparaging smile crept across his handsome face, and he shook his head at my temper. 'I wouldn't say the flowers and bonbons were wasted. The nuts, I see, failed to charm. And speaking of nuts, Lady Red will be waiting for us.'

'I would really like to go home now, please.'

'I shall make your apologies to Lady Red. May I tell her you'll be back tomorrow?'

'You've gotten what you wanted from me. If anyone delivers a bag of old banknotes to my door, you may be sure I'll send them on to you, Mr Maitland.'

'I would appreciate that, Miss Haley. And incidentally, they weren't old banknotes; they were crisp, brand-new ones. Unmarked, too, as the locks don't care to have their fees fiddled with. But it isn't just information I want from you.'

'What else, then?'

He reached across the ledgers and took my hand. The old laughing mischief was gone from his eyes. He looked serious, even grave. 'I want to be Desmond again. I want you to be Belle. Unlike some people, I have nothing against mixing business and pleasure. It has been a great pleasure doing business with you. You know how ill the business end of our relationship has fared. The pleasure wasn't in that. I wish we had met in some other way, but I would rather have met you like this than not have met you at all. It's hard for an old sinner like me to have the memory of a saint for competition, Belle. Give me a little time to grapple with it.'

The breath caught in my throat, and I felt a warmth around my collar. I looked down at my lap and saw his long fingers clasping mine. His fingers moved, and one hand rose to tilt my chin up till we were gazing at each other. I knew by the soft, lambent glow in his eyes he was going to kiss me, right there in broad daylight in his carriage. Graham would have been scandalized.

'Desmond, I . . .'

'Hush!'

His lips brushed mine, lightly as a breeze. I heard a faint gasp, knew it was mine, then forgot it as his lips firmed and his arms went around me in a crushing embrace. I heard the ledgers hit the floor—I think he pushed them off the seat on purpose to be closer to me. It was unthinkable that I, the tyrant of Bath, was allowing this to happen. I made an ineffectual effort to push him away but found my fingers weakening to water, then moving around his neck. I felt the exciting bristle of rough hair under my fingers, felt his lips bruising mine, and became aware that my body was turning to a quivering blancmange in his arms. Kissing Graham had never been like this. This violent chemistry was something else entirely. His lips were a spark to the dry tinder of my being, and the flame showed some sign of burning out of control.

For all my preaching propriety, it was Desmond who brought it to a halt. He pulled away and looked wild-eyed at what had happened between us. 'Belle, forgive me. I shouldn't have—' He sounded aghast.

I may be a Bath Miss, but at least I am not a hypocrite, and I had no intention of laying the whole blame in his dish. 'It's no matter. It won't happen again.' My brave words were rendered quite ludicrous by the breathless voice in which they were uttered. I had never felt such a fool in my life, but I had been struck nearly dumb by that ruthless embrace.

He just went on looking in a strange, incredulous way. I busied myself picking up the ledgers, and he felt obliged to help, as he had knocked them off on purpose. When the battered books had been replaced in the carton with as much care as though they were a stack of priceless Gutenberg Bibles, we sat back and tried to think of something to say to break the tension. I looked down at my shoes, out the window, and finally up at the clouds, but from the corner of my eye I saw Desmond staring at me.

At last I could take it no more and glared at him. 'That's better,' he said, and smiled nervously. 'I've had the cut infernal, the cut indirect, and even the cut sublime. That baleful glare is a relief, I can tell you.'

'What are you talking about?'

'More cant, but this one is less reprehensible. At Cambridge, where I studied, there is a system of renouncing acquaintances by staring at other things while meeting them. Each has varying degrees of opprobrium. You spared me the cut direct, for which I thank you. No doubt that will come the first time we meet on the street.'

'You are making much to-do about nothing. I'm not angry at all.'

'Then why are you refusing to visit Lady Red? Come on, Belle, think of the poor thing, shivering in the cold, starving, waiting for her nuts. She probably has a litter to feed.' As he wheedled he pulled a bag of nuts from the side pocket of the carriage.

'You're the most unconscionable rogue in

London, Desmond Maitland. You'd sink to any depths, even using an innocent animal to get your own way. Let us go, then, before the brood dies of malnutrition. I expect you've completely spoiled her for foraging. She'll be sitting on her fat haunches, waiting for you to serve her. How does it come you don't bring a silver platter?'

He relaxed into a normal smile. 'I tried it. She prefers my fingers.' He pulled the check string again, and at the first corner the carriage turned toward Hyde Park.

The remainder of the afternoon passed pleasantly, with no further mention of K. Norman, Graham, the infamous kiss, or the missing money. Desmond told me about himself, his being only a younger son, but one who was fortunate enough to have a wealthy uncle who left him an unspecified sum of money, which he used to establish himself as an underwriting merchant at Lloyd's. I regaled him with the tedium of my days at Bath but didn't mention how Graham had changed all that.

'Less and less can I understand your eagerness to sell the house and return to Bath,' he said, shaking out the last of the nuts on to the grass.

'Bath may be dull, but at least it's a known evil. It takes courage to change for the unknown. Besides, it's not only myself. There's Mama and Esther to consider as well.'

'You don't strike me as a lady lacking in courage. What the three of you need is a husband—each, I mean.'

'I didn't think you meant we should share one. I doubt very much that our tastes would be similar enough for one to please us all.'

'What sort of gentleman would please you, Belle?' He realized as soon as he had said it that my choice had already been established with Graham. I could tell by the quick frown that he regretted the question, and I decided to put him out of his discomfort.

'When you reach my advanced state of decrepitude, you cannot be particular. I mean to give Mama a run for Mr Stone's affections. That's why she rouged her cheeks! Desmond, I bet he's calling this afternoon. She was as nervous as a kitten. I know she didn't put on her best lace collar only to impress the modiste. And Esther was very skittish, too. That wretched Duke will be there as well. I must get home!'

He was amused at my concern, but he called the carriage. 'I can't be sponsor for Mr Stone's intentions, but I assure you Duke is a decent fellow. He's already wondering whether Miss Esther would prefer a diamond engagement ring or sapphires to match her eyes.'

'She's only seventeen years old!'

'He's only twenty-four.'

'Yes, but he's—oh, you know,' I worried. 'Can't these nags go any faster?'

He gave the groom some signal by jiggling the check string, and before long we were raffling through the streets at a breakneck pace. I was right to have been worried, too. Both Mr Stone and Duke were in the saloon, drinking Graham's wine—one empty bottle sat on its side on the table with a small puddle of wine dripping from its mouth, and another was nearly empty, giving the scene a disreputable air. They were eating Desmond's bonbons and nuts, laughing and talking most foolishly while a table of cards sat abandoned. Plans were afoot for all manner of outings—a play, a drive in the country, and, to assuage Mama's conscience, a return to St Paul's. Really it was the nature of the conversation that displeased me most. Mr Stone spoke quite openly of mistresses and lightskirts and something called the Green Room at the theater, which sounded a very den of iniquity. Mama looked quite shocked, but she didn't do a thing to stop him. She wouldn't know how, the innocent soul. I think even Desmond, who was hardly a stern moralist, was surprised to see such familiar carrying on.

In a voice that would freeze an Eskimo, I pointed out the hour, and the fact that we had to clear away the mess and prepare our own dinner. It was actually not late at all, but no one had the courage to tell me so. Finally Mr Stone got to his feet. 'I'll call on you tomorrow, then, Bridget,' he said on his way out the door. He had battered down Mama's defenses. The rector, Mr Strong had been hinting for six months to call her Bridget and had always met with a simpering put-off.

Once Stone was gone, I didn't mind calling her to order in front of Duke and Desmond. 'Mama, I'm surprised at you! You hardly know that old man, and to let him talk so broad in front of Esther! Look at this mess—sluicing wine and gossiping. Don't pretend there was any serious discussion going on here.'

She looked properly chastened and tried to appease me by saying our gowns would be ready in a few days. 'I don't care about the gowns. I have a good mind to take the pair of you home to Bath at the crack of dawn tomorrow.'

'But Hotchkiss and Ettie arrive tomorrow, Belle,' she pointed out. 'You cannot load them back on the coach the very day they arrive. You know how tired and shaken we were when we reached London.'

Duke cast a look of terror at me but firmed himself up to do battle. 'Just telling your mother, Miss Haley—ought to wait till spring. Deuced hard traveling in winter. Snowbanks, roads a regular hasty pudding.'

'I prefer snowbanks and bad roads to Mr Stone.'

'Mr Stone is Duke's uncle, dear,' Mama warned me, with an apologetic smile at Duke.

I gave Duke a withering stare and said, 'I

140

am quite aware of that fact.'

'Only on my mama's side,' Duke offered in atonement. 'I ain't a Stone myself.'

I said not a word about blocks or blockheads.

Desmond got a hand on his friend's elbow and began leading him toward the front door. Duke's protestations were quite audible. 'Woman's a dashed shrew.' Desmond pulled him along faster. 'Don't know how you can call her an Incomparable. Regular Tartar.'

Desmond pushed Duke into the hall and turned to make his adieux. 'Good afternoon, ladies. Thank you for your help, Belle. I'll drop around—er—before you leave?' There was more laughter than fear or chagrin in his flashing black orbs.

'Then you had better make it very soon. Good day.'

They left, but within ten seconds the knocker sounded, and Des was back with the carton of ledgers. 'You *did* say to come back soon,' he pointed out. 'Don't bite my nose off. Duke has just been prophesying you'll break my spine in three places and snap off my nose. He thinks me a very brave soul to have entered a carriage alone with you. When can we do it again? You aren't *really* leaving very soon, are you?'

'I'm much too upset to decide anything. Just put those on the table, please. I don't know what you must think of us after coming into

141

such a scene of debauchery.'

'I come to think your Mama and Esther and I would deal famously. You're the last holdout, Belle.'

'You'll have to be satisfied with bigamy.'

'I'd settle for monogamy, if it were the right mono. I don't mean mono-tony.' I clenched my lips to restrain a smile, but he misunderstood it. 'I'll let you back to your duties. Give 'em hell.' He smiled and whisked out the door, laughing.

I stayed alone in the hall a minute to compose myself. I had overreacted to Mama's little dissipation. It was as much the shock as anything else that accounted for it. To see your own mother flirting with an old roue, and in front of her young and impressionable daughter, was most annoying. To be perfectly truthful, I would have been less angry had Desmond not been witness to the scene, after my having given him a good Bear Garden jaw for his lax morals.

Actually, I had done worse than either Mama or Esther. I had allowed that scamp to kiss me in broad daylight. The whole Haley family was on the road to disrepute, and to judge by the snickering giggles from the saloon, they were enjoying it thoroughly. The glowing image reflected in the mirror told me my own aversion to vice was not so strong as it should be, either. I was thinking of Duke's protest. 'Don't know how you can call her an

142

Incomparable.'

I schooled my features to anger and returned to the saloon.

CHAPTER NINE

That evening, Eliot dropped in around nine to report that he had delivered the parcel to the home for retired clerics, where it had been very welcome. He didn't stay long—it was a courtesy call only. I wanted a little private conversation with him, and when he pulled out his watch—Graham's watch that I had given to him—I rose to accompany him to the door.

'You don't know how I treasure this timepiece,' he said, gazing at it and rubbing his finger over the glass. 'It was thoughtful of you to give it to me.'

'I'm glad you like it.'

'It is not a question of liking; it is the original owner, and more particularly the donor, that makes me cherish it.'

This was accompanied by an admiring glance at me. In the hall he espied the stack of ledgers, which led naturally to the business I wanted to discuss. 'Where did these come from?' he asked.

I knew his poor opinion of Mr Maitland, and to prevent any disagreeableness I said only that Mr Sinclair had given them to me. 'These last bits of business must be attended to while I am here. The odd thing is, Eliot, that there is no mention of K. Norman in the ledgers.'

'But there wouldn't be, Belle. It wasn't a business expense. Graham paid Norman out of his own pocket.'

'You mentioned some large case Graham had won. That isn't in the ledgers either. All his cases were small.'

His noble brow creased while he considered this oddity, but eventually he figured out the mystery. 'I see what it is now. He handled a case for an uncle of his—old Elmer Sutton from Norfolk. It had to do with some neighbor trying to diddle Elmer out of a strip of land. Graham wouldn't take a fee for it—you know Graham! He never put self-interest before family. But Elmer insisted on rewarding him all the same and gave him a thousand pounds. It seems Graham considered it a gift or inheritance, not a fee, so he didn't enter it in his business ledger.'

'When did this occur?'

'It was just before you and Graham became involved, I believe. That's why you didn't hear of it.'

'But I didn't see any such deposit in his personal bank account either.'

'We can only conjecture, but he probably decided against depositing it. I know he mentioned that Elmer—he's quite an eccentric—paid him in golden boys from his own vault. Very likely Graham kept on hand the cash he didn't give directly to Norman and used it for expense money. And, of course, as soon as Graham met you he began looking about for a house and furnishings and so on. I remember he paid for many things in gold sovereigns. Something of the sort must be the explanation, as you say there's no record of the transaction anywhere.'

'Yes, that would account for it. It's not important, but I just wondered, you know.'

'As you said, you're clearing up all the odds and ends. There is one detail I was to arrange for you. About Graham's carriage, Belle— when do you want me to hire a team and get it out of storage for you?'

I was torn on that matter. 'A carriage would certainly be convenient in town, but on the other hand, till I sell the house, I don't like to take on the added expense. Perhaps I'll just sell the carriage.'

'Why don't I hitch up my team and bring the carriage around for your inspection? There are two advantages. It will give you a chance to decide whether you want to hold on to it till you leave and take it to Bath with you. It's a very pretty rig.'

'Yes, it's much nicer than our own family carriage. And what is the other advantage?'

He gave a slow, intimate smile and said, 'It gives me an unexceptionable opportunity to drive out with you.'

That smile was attractive enough to unsettle me. 'If you wouldn't mind bringing it around . . .?'

'Mind? Belle, how could I mind doing it for you?' he asked, and shook his head. 'You bruise my feelings, showing this reluctance to use me. Nothing pleases me more than being able to do a few errands for you.'

'You're very kind. I'll just run upstairs and get the letter from the solicitor, then.'

'You'll have to write a letter to the stable as well, giving me permission to act for you. Just a few lines. I'll wait.'

When I returned from dashing off the letter Eliot was taking a glance through Graham's ledgers. 'I believe Graham made a mistake in setting up his shop on Jermyn Street. He would have gotten more interesting cases had he paid a higher rent in a more fashionable district. Real estate and wills—Graham was capable of more than that.'

'He made a fair income, though.'

'He worked hard for it. A regular demon for work.'

'Here are the letters. When will you bring the carriage?'

'I wish I could say tomorrow morning, but my trip to the country . . . It's a wedding, or I'd put the trip off and get the carriage first. Can you wait three days?' I nodded my approval. 'Oh, by the way, I dropped around to Fleury Lane. There's no longer a K. Norman living

146

there. No one even remembers him. It's the kind of neighborhood where people are moving all the time. Little better than hovels, really. Not the sort of place I should like to think of you going to. I'd be uneasy all day, worrying about you. You won't go, will you, Belle?'

I was flattered at his concern. 'I have no intention of going. Thank you for all your help, Eliot. You must come to dinner after our servants arrive and make us respectable.'

'I look forward to it. Good night, Belle.' I reached to shake his hand, but he lifted my fingers to his lips and kissed them. As he bent over my hand I saw his face at an odd angle, with the widow's peak and high brow thrown into prominence. Such an odd sensation, as though it were Graham. I waited for the old familiar lump to rise up in my throat. It didn't happen. I enjoyed the unaccustomed flattery of a man kissing my fingers, but I did not feel it was Graham come back to me. I was coming to appreciate Eliot for himself.

After he left, I took the ledgers and added them to the carton of items to be thrown out. Eliot and Graham were both in my mind. Graham was the worthier man, but Eliot was undeniably more attractive. Graham slaved all day in that lithe cubbyhole of an office, and he didn't even have to. He had an income, whereas Eliot lived a butterfly existence. Nevertheless, the butterfly was very kind and

147

courteous to me. A little more than kind, really.

The mood in the saloon was so sullen when I rejoined the family that the tyrant admitted her plans to remain in London, but she laid down some pretty stiff rules of conduct for her mother. She was not to drive out alone with Mr Stone nor to entertain him without myself to chaperon them. We retired early and spent the morning cleaning house for the arrival of the servants. Hotchkiss was not demanding, but Ettie would be disillusioned with us if she found any dust on what would soon be called 'her' tables.

The servants came at noon and bustled noisily about. After delivering a fairly extensive diatribe on the evils of coach travel, they had to decide whether or not they approved of the house. 'A regular shoebox is what it is!' Ettie told me. 'How that Mr Sutton ever expected you to live in four rooms is above and beyond me!'

'He didn't, Ettie. He expected me to make use of the upstairs as well as down.'

'Fine talking, miss, but where are me and Hotchkiss expected to lay our heads? That attic is like an icehouse, and there's no beds neither.'

'Esther and I will move into the master bedroom. You and Hotchkiss will have the rooms we are using at present.'

'Sleep on the same floor as the family?' she

asked, outraged.

'We won't bite you. It is only for a week at the most.'

'There's a deal of linen to be changed, then, and all the unpacking to do. I'll get at it and send Hotchkiss out for real food.'

Ettie was a fan of square meals, preferably a roasted joint large enough to feed an army, which means it feeds a small family for half a week.

Mr Stone came to call in the afternoon as threatened. 'I've left the carriage standing by, Bridget,' he said, and cast a sheepish eye at her.

'You had best tell your groom to drive along,' I informed him stiffly. 'My mother wishes to remain at home this afternoon.'

He glared at me from his bloodshot eyes but sent word to his groom before taking a seat and looking around for a bottle of wine. 'Would you care for a cup of tea, Mr Stone?' I asked.

'Eh? I could use something to take off the chill.' His eyes wavered to the wine table.

'Fine, I'll call for tea,' I said, and pulled the rope.

At two-thirty Mr Duke was added to our party, and he accepted a cup of tepid tea, for I did not call for a new pot. Duke was completely terrified of me. He sat silent as a Trappist monk, though his expression was less resigned than frustrated. He never glanced at the wine table at all. He scarcely even dared to roll his eyes at Esther. I was sure such Turkish treatment would shorten their visit, but when Yootha landed in at three, my rule was at an end.

'We'll want fresh tea, Belle,' Mama ventured.

'Tea? Don't trouble your servants with tea, Mrs Haley. Wine will do fine for me. Ah, Esther! I see you have attached yourself a fine young beau. Didn't I tell you how it would be? And you, you old reprobate,' she said, turning to Mr Stone. 'I hope you are behaving yourself!'

'I'll help you to wine, Mrs Mailer,' he said, and jumped up to fill two glasses. He brought the bottle to the table and made great inroads into it. Duke looked longingly at the bottle, fearfully at me, and sipped his tea.

'Well, you are all very dull, I must say,' Yootha remarked when I began extolling the virtues of St Paul's. 'Shall we have a hand of cards to pass the time?'

The table was hauled out, I was required to fill the fourth seat, and Duke at last got hold of the wine and some privacy with Esther. The conversation at the card table involved gowns, parties, personalities, and such elevated gossip. The only pleasing aspect to it was that I won rather a lot of money: a pound note from Mr Stone, who didn't resent it, and a shilling from Yootha, who did.

I was just ushering them out the door, though Mr Duke still clung to the sofa like a barnacle, when Mr Maitland came pouncing in. He exchanged curt greetings with the parting guests. I could see that Desmond was excited about something, and it wasn't a happy excitement. Mama busied herself tidying up the card table while I led him to the sofa across the room from Esther and Duke to gain some semblance of privacy. I doubted the others could hear our talk over Esther's giggling. Mr Duke was beginning to find some favor in that quarter.

'Have you seen Eliot Sutton today?' he asked.

'No, he's out of town. Why do you ask?'

'Whereabouts?'

'I don't know. He had to attend a country wedding. Why do you want to see him?'

'No special reason. I thought he might throw some light on this business of Graham's ledgers. The two of them were close as inkle weavers.'

'I asked him about the ledgers,' I said, and explained why the entries were not there.

He listened with sharp interest, but when he spoke it was about another aspect of the matter. 'I see! He *has* been to call, then!' A quick flash of suspicion shone in his eyes.

'He came by last night,' I said, suddenly angry with myself for feeling I had to explain anything to this impertinent stranger. 'I expect to see him again tomorrow. He is attending to a personal matter for me.'

'What personal matter?' he demanded.

'Personal means one's own private affair, Desmond. May I know why you've developed this sudden interest in Eliot?'

He put on a conning smile and tried to get around me. 'Now, you must know I am interested in any gentleman who is trying to cut me out with the shrew.' Duke apparently overheard the last word, for he darted a frightened glance at us, expecting me to go into a rant. I smiled at him very sweetly to let him know I didn't plan to assassinate anyone.

'I have no time to think of romance.'

'I deem it a mistake for any unmarried lady to let herself become that busy. Let me share your labors. It is not having a carriage and your stubborn refusal to use mine that is keeping you too busy for romance. I believe you inherited Mr Sutton's carriage. Why don't I hire you a team and have it brought around for your use?'

'Thank you, but that is already being taken care of.'

'Would you call that a very personal, private affair?' he asked, and laughed. I had the feeling he had known all along what matter Eliot was handling for me and had needed only to confirm it.

'How did you find out?'

'I went to the stable and tried for a look at

the rig. I know Graham was on horseback the night—that night, but I thought he might possibly have hidden the money there. It was a long shot. They refused me permission to see the carriage, but I know you will inform me if you find a pleasant bulge in a side pocket.'

'But Eliot's not retrieving the carriage till tomorrow.'

'Yes, that's what they said. His groom had been around with your letter and orders to have it cleaned up for duty. And other than the heavy burden of issuing that order to Eliot, what has kept you too busy for romance?'

'Trying to bring this brood of mine to respectability. I want you to know I was a perfect ogre all afternoon.'

'Some traces of it still linger.'

'I kept the wine bottle closed—well, at least till Aunt Yootha arrived.'

'Aunt Yootha? Surely she was Graham's aunt, not yours?'

'That's true, but in the family we were in the habit of calling her Aunt Yootha. We have known her for eons at home.'

'Now that Yootha's uncorked the bottle . . .' He looked to the sofa table, where there was still one drink left.

'Help yourself.'

'Shall I help you, too? We'll need another bottle.'

'It's in the cellar. Hotchkiss is out shopping, and Ettie is changing linens. It's too much bother.'

'Come along, lazybones. I'll go down with you and help you select.' He helped me up from the sofa and we got a candle to go downstairs.

'I hope you don't think we are always so informal, Desmond. I usually run a tighter ship, but with this move we're all at sixes and sevens. Here we are,' I said as we reached the cellar landing.

Desmond walked down the aisle, lifting an occasional bottle to read the label. 'You have some good stuff here.'

'Rum goods, Grant called them.'

'I was careful to avoid the vernacular, as you had an aversion to it. Slang is strangely seductive, though—I've heard even bishops use it.' He set the candle on a barrel and lifted a dusty bottle. 'I wonder where he got hold of this claret. An excellent vintage.'

'Eliot could tell you. He was Graham's mentor in the wine department. Eliot managed to get these racks from some house that was being wrecked. He suggested putting the racks here, too, away from the window draft.'

His nostrils pinched in, but he managed to control his sneer and settle for mere sarcasm instead. 'Then I shan't dare to tell you they ought to be farther away from drafts, where the temperature is more stable. I am beginning to learn that Eliot's word is not to be trifled with. Do you think Eliot would permit our sharing this bottle?' he asked.

'He is only my friend, not my master.'

'A very good friend, Belle?' he asked, staring through the shadows at me. 'Have you known him a long time?'

'I never met him before this visit. He must have visited Yootha in Bath, but I never chanced to meet him.'

'He is a completely new acquaintance, then?'

'Yes, but the friendship was hastened along because of his being Graham's cousin and friend. They are very similar—in looks, I mean.'

'Looks can deceive.'

'I am not deceived regarding Eliot. I know he's a butterfly, but butterflies can be charming. And even useful—he's been helpful to us in many ways.'

'What ways were these?'

The cellar was an odd place to choose for a conversation, but it gave us privacy, and neither of us made any move to leave.

'He took Graham's personal effects away for us; he's going to bring his carriage around tomorrow. Oh, and incidentally, he checked out Fleury Lane for me, too. K. Norman is no longer there.'

There was a long, uncomfortable pause. A disbelieving pause, somehow. Desmond looked on the verge of saying something, of

155

contradicting me.

'Why do you look like that? Did you go to Fleury Lane, too?'

'I did, but, like Eliot, I found nothing to report. I'm sorry if I've been hard on Eliot. You know where to lay the blame.' He looked at me from the corner of his eye with a quizzical expression.

'Shall we go back up now?'

'We had better, before I do something you will dislike.'

I turned and took a step away. His fingers gripped my arm and brought me to a stop. My heart began pounding, and I knew—thought I knew—what he was about. He turned me around and looked at me for a long, silent moment in the flickering candlelight. Then he smiled and said, 'Don't worry. I'm not going to kiss you. Not now.'

What a contrary man he was! He laughed lightly and picked up the candle, and we returned to the saloon. Duke was behaving with perfect propriety, though Mama, the peagoose, had left the two youngsters unattended.

Esther had wound him around her thumb. 'Duke says he'll take us all to the Haymarket as soon as we get our gowns. They should be ready tomorrow. Can we go tomorrow night, Belle?'

'Why are you asking me? You must ask Mama.'

'You know she won't let us go if you don't allow it.'

'Who exactly comprises this party, Mr Duke?' I inquired stiffly.

Duke had obviously given no thought to the matter. 'Esther, me, you, of course . . .'

'You feel up to escorting three ladies, do you, Duke?' Desmond asked, but his quick glance in my direction hinted at the one he might hesitate to tackle.

'I thought maybe you . . . Uncle Charles . . . Dash it, there are six seats in the box. We might as well fill them all up, as we'll be paying for them.'

'I accept,' Des said, 'but does Miss Haley accept the inclusion of Mr Stone in the party?'

I was nearly as eager for the trip as Esther, and it seemed hard to deny Mama her flirt when Esther and I were secure of ours. Three pairs of hopeful, curious eyes stared at me, awaiting my decision. 'Good gracious, Mama is old enough to decide for herself. You must ask her, Esther.'

Esther bolted off and was back before you could say Jack Robinson to announce Mama's agreement. A new mood of merriment descended on us, as will so often happen at the anticipation of a delightful indiscretion. Esther brought out the cards, and we all sat around playing Pope Joan for shillings. We only played for pennies at home, and I was convinced that the gentlemen, who beat Esther and me quite

157

mercilessly, would not demand their winnings.

I misjudged their gallantry. Desmond reached out his hand when we called the game over. My winnings from Mr Stone were completely wiped out. I had to pay not only the pound note but another two shillings as well.

'That's twice today I've disappointed you,' Desmond said as he pocketed the money.

I knew he referred to the episode in the cellar but could not permit him to think so. 'Yes, indeed, but my disappointment at your accepting the invitation to the Haymarket palls beside having to pay out hard cash. That really hurts.'

He jiggled the end of my nose with his finger and said, 'I just want to keep you on your toes. I don't want you to feel you know me too thoroughly. Familiarity breeds contempt.'

Duke was nonplussed at such daring as Desmond's actually touching me. He looked wildly at Esther. I began to lead Desmond to the door. 'How true. One cannot help feeling contempt at a gentleman's taking familiar privileges with a lady's nose.'

'Thank you for the advice. Next time I shall lower my familiarity an inch. I received no lecture for trespassing on your lips.'

'Some familiarities are, of course, beneath contempt.'

'Very true; the more pleasant familiarities

are quite unspeakable. Speaking of the unspeakable, shall I haul Duke along with me? He'll be here till midnight if I don't.'

'Please take him. Is he really all right, Desmond? I thought Esther was only amusing herself with him, but I have noticed a rather soft smile on her this afternoon. It's all your fault for telling her he is sought after.'

'She couldn't do better. Charles Stone is another matter. I'd be wary of any crony of Prinny's. We'll keep a sharp eye on them tomorrow night at the theater. Shall I send my carriage around tomorrow morning for you, or will Eliot have finally attended to bringing your own? You must have any amount of shopping and sightseeing to do.'

'I have a strong feeling Mr Duke will put himself and his carriage at Esther's disposal. It shan't leave the door without me in it.'

He shook his head in dismay. 'So lavish of your presence with the one man in London who will dislike it intensely. I'll drop by in the afternoon in case Duke disappoints you. I don't expect you to stay home, but I'll drop around to check.'

'Thank you. I don't know yet what tomorrow might bring.'

'That's what makes life interesting, isn't it? Who would have thought last week that the mail coach from Bath would deliver such unexpected delights?' He stopped and a slow smile crept across his lips, wrinkling the corners of his eyes. 'Now I'm going to kiss you, Belle,' he warned. His hands reached for me. I evaded them and darted back to the saloon to tell Mr Duke his friend was waiting for him.

'No need. I have my own buggy,' Duke said.

'It is waiting as well.'

'Eh? I didn't send for it.'

'I did.'

'Oh. Thank you very much, Miss Haley. Very kind of you.' With a baleful glare, he waddled from the room.

From behind he looked like a knock-kneed badger. I was amazed that Esther would give him the time of day, but there is no accounting for taste. It was even stranger that the tall gallant waiting for his friend would find anything of delight in me, yet it didn't seem possible the laughing glow in his eyes was simulated.

Desmond smiled and said, 'We'll continue our—er—discussion next time, Belle. Good day.'

The evening seemed very flat, with all our friends having forsaken us. A dozen times I went to the window, sure that one of the passing carriages would stop and a visitor come to our door. Nothing of the sort happened. The only liveliness in our evening was Ettie's bustling about the house. She came to check that Esther and I had what we needed when we went up to the master bedroom, which we were now sharing.

'You'll see a wee bit of an ivory painting there on the bedside table,' she told me. 'I found it under the pillow when I made up the bed fresh for you. A pretty little thing. Must be some kin to Mr Sutton, as he had it under his pillow.'

I went to look at it immediately and found myself staring at a very lovely young face. It was a miniature on ivory of a blond girl I had never seen before in my life.

'Let me see!' Esther said, crowding at my elbow. 'Pretty!' Actually, she bore a resemblance to Esther—not a striking resemblance, but she was the same type and age. 'Who can she be?'

'I have no idea.'

'You must know! Graham had it under his pillow. Perhaps he had a light o' love, Belle,' she said, and laughed, for of course we both believed such dissipation entirely unlikely of Graham. 'Mama might know. Why don't you ask her?'

I asked Mama, who was as much perplexed as I. She murmured, 'Very strange, very strange indeed. Almost as though . . . but Graham was not *that* sort of gentleman.'

'Don't be ridiculous. Of course he wasn't.'

'According to Mr Stone, they all do it in London. A fellow is considered very dull if he doesn't have a mistress. That's what he said.'

'Do you think Mr Stone considers himself dull, Mama?' I asked. Though it was a rhetorical question asked to open up her eyes, she was at pains to assure me that he called himself a dull old lad.

I did not consider Graham dull by any means, but neither did I believe he had a mistress. It was preposterous. Yet as I lay in bed thinking about it I could come up with no other possible explanation. It was the fact of the thing being under his pillow that defeated me. My likeness was on his desk. This one was even closer to him. And she was so very, very pretty. Yootha or Eliot might be able to enlighten me, but I did not think I would show the miniature to them. I regretted that Esther had seen it. Because if the unthinkable was true and Graham had been unfaithful to me, I preferred to keep the secret locked in my own heart. But I would not believe it; I would rather live in doubt than have to acknowledge that Graham was untrue.

CHAPTER TEN

After a poor night's rest, I woke in the morning feeling like a dishrag. The trip to the Haymarket Theatre loomed as an ordeal. Even the arrival of our gowns from the modiste failed to cheer me, though they were lovely. In my skirt pocket the ivory miniature, not an inch wide by two inches long, burdened me as though it were a block of lead. There was some tacit agreement among the family that the find would not be discussed, which didn't stop Esther and Mama from casting pitying glances at me.

Eliot would not be coming today. As my rough treatment had kept Mr Stone and Duke at bay, the only company to be looked forward to was that of Desmond's groom, who was to bring the carriage around in the afternoon. To disperse my fit of the dismals, I decided to accept the use of it, just this once, and take Mama and Esther to Hyde Park at four o'clock to gawk at the *ton*.

We were ready by three, except to put on our pelisses, and we sat in state in the saloon, awaiting the carriage. When the wheels drew to a stop Desmond hopped out and paced toward our door. He had someone with him— a man who did not quite merit the term 'gentleman' yet who looked a notch above the 'coves.' My low spirits rose insensibly, and when Hotchkiss went to the door I felt a smile lift my lips. My fingers closed around the ivory miniature, and I knew I would show it to Desmond.

Then he was announced, and my plan was forgotten. I stared in wonder at the implacable face he wore, the stiff bow, the angry lines that pinched his lips to white, and, worst of all, the black accusation in his eyes.

'Desmond, what is it?' I demanded.

He didn't say a word but only stared at me as though I were a she-devil. It was his companion who spoke, and I shall never forget the fear that seized my heart, clenching it into a hard, cold stone. The man held out a piece of paper and announced, 'I have a search warrant for these premises, Miss Haley. I am an officer of the law, and any interference in the execution of my duty will be considered a misdemeanor.'

A trembling seized me. I was quite sure I was going to faint, till Mama beat me to it. To make matters worse, she was standing at the time, and she reeled over on to the floor with an dreadful thump. My trembling ceased, my heart unfroze, and once more the blood coursed through my veins. I grabbed the wine bottle and ran to Mama while Esther darted off for Ettie. Hotchkiss came pelting in, and among the lot of us we got Mama lifted to the sofa.

While we did this the intruders stood uncertainly, but they did not offer help or even apologize. When they had ascertained that Mama was recovering, the officer of the law announced that we were not to leave the house or remove so much as a handkerchief under penalty of I hardly know what—hanging, perhaps.

They marched upstairs, where they began rooting through all our private things. Hotchkiss announced, with fire in his eyes, 'I'll just run up and keep a guard on them. They won't fill their pockets—not if I know anything!'

'I'll get my butcher knife and have that lad's gizzard out if he goes meddling with my privates,' Ettie declared. 'The bare-faced traitor! And him sitting in your saloon, miss, guzzling your wine all yesterday afternoon.'

When Mama was able to speak she asked in a faint, quavering voice, 'What does it mean, Belle? What is he looking for?'

'The money, of course,' I told her.

'What makes him think it's here?' Esther demanded. Soon she was lamenting, 'I suppose this means we shan't be going to the Haymarket this evening.'

My first bout of fear was stiffening to anger. How dare Desmond Maitland accuse us of being thieves, after all the help we had given him? He had ruined our day, but he would not ruin Esther's longed-for trip to the theater. 'If we're not locked up in Bridewell by that time, we shall go, Esther,' I promised her. 'I can guarantee, however, that Mr Maitland will not be of the party.'

'And he seemed so very nice,' Mama said, shaking her head sadly. 'It was all a con, Belle. He has only been pretending to have a tendre for you to gain access to this house. All along he thought we were thieves. Say what you will about Mr Stone. He would never do anything like this.'

I could hardly control the angry shaking of my voice. 'No human being would do such a thing! The man is an ogre. I shall never forgive this, never!'

Mama, that mountain of understatement, allowed that it went 'beyond anything. Really, it is nothing less than a betrayal of friendship.'

'I wish Duke were here,' Esther murmured. As though that little badger could have stood up to a monster like Maitland.

When they had finished with the upstairs they returned below, still with Hotchkiss glaring and Ettie glowering, the butcher knife clutched under her apron and a Bible in her other hand to ward off these twin demons. We ladies went upstairs to get as far away from them as we could. We all huddled, scared to death, in the master bedroom. It bore a few traces of their meddling but was not seriously disarranged.

We talked desultorily at first, but as time passed we all fell silent, which allowed me to think. Why had Maitland suddenly changed his tactics? He had already searched this house from rafters to cellar and knew there was no money here. What had happened to change his mind? Did he think I had secreted the money elsewhere and brought it back after his search? If this were so—and I could find no other explanation—then he had thought all along that I was a common thief, and his acting the gallant had been just that—an act. How had he convinced a judge to swear out a warrant?

It was close to an hour later when Ettie came to the door and said Officer Roy would like to speak to Miss Haley in the saloon.

'Oh, dear, do you think you should go?' Mama asked. Her pale little face was pinched in anguish for me. 'Do you want us to go with you, Belle?'

I knew what an ordeal it would be for her, and I wished to spare Esther as well. 'Of course I must go, but there's no need for you to bother. I intend to have an apology from Officer Roy before he leaves. At least Mr Maitland has left.' I looked questioningly at Ettie.

'He was just putting on his hat when I came up,' she assured me.

'Good, then I'll go. I am curious to learn why this search was made. I'll find out from Officer Roy.'

The officer was alone in the saloon, but I saw through the curtains that Maitland's carriage was waiting for him. I strode in with my head high and a martial temper displayed on my face. Roy jumped to his feet when he got a look at me.

'I would like an explanation and an apology for this unforgivable intrusion, sir.' He pointed to the sofa, but I chose to remain on my feet. I was much too excited to sit.

'It was the money, you see, miss,' he began very conciliatory.

'So I gathered. What convinced Mr Maitland that it was here when he had already searched the house from top to bottom?'

He handed me a crisp, new pound note and said, 'This here is what convinced him.'

Did he find it here?' I asked.

'Not exactly find it. The story I got is that you gave it to him yourself, Miss Haley. Maitland set up a game of cards and arranged to win so as to see a sample of your blunt, like. This here is the bill you gave him, and it's part and parcel of the lot that was stolen.'

I remembered discussing the bills with Maitland. *They were crisp, brand-new ones. Unmarked, too . . .'*

'How does he know this is a part of the stolen money? He said the bills weren't marked.'

I daresay he said that to fool you. They're not marked so as you'd notice, but if you look close, there's a little cut there halfway down the left side. He didn't even do it on purpose, for the locks don't care for marked money, but when the bills came from the Mint he happened to notice that bit of an irregularity. You'll see as well that although this here bill is two years old, it hasn't been circulated. We figure it was sitting in the case all the while, keeping fresh.'

'That strikes me as very slim evidence on which to have sworn out a warrant to search my house.'

'Well, 'tis and 'tisn't. In his work, Maitland often has to deal with the judges, and they've come to see he usually knows what he's talking about. He generally sniffs the wind from the right direction,' he added, eying me askance.

'He erred this time.'

'Did he?' His blue eyes, sharp with suspicion, bore into me.

'Yes, he did.'

He leaned closer and spoke in a low tone. 'He's ready to deal soft with you, miss. My advice is, leap at it. Just tell us where we can pick up the rest of it, and it won't go no farther. You'll be saved the shame of arrest and the downright disagreeableness of being locked up. Nasty place, Bridewell.'

In the unlikely event that you have ever swallowed a white hot coal, you will understand how I felt. My breast burned; my head felt as if it would burst. I pointed my finger at the door and shouted like a fishwife. 'Get out! Get out of my house, and don't you ever dare to darken this door again! I'll have you reported to the Prime Minister. And you can tell Mr Maitland he has sniffed the wind from the wrong direction this time. His little comedy failed to work.'

The officer shook his head and clicked his tongue. 'Where did you get this note, then, miss?' He waved the cursed pound note before my eyes.

I had to commit some act of violence, and

since I was afraid to strike an officer of the law, I snatched the banknote and ran for the grate. He stopped me before I could chuck it into the flames. 'I don't know where it came from. It's his word against mine that I gave it to him.'

'That's your last word, then?'

'Yes.'

Officer Roy stood, feet apart, and nodded his head. 'Burning up that bit of evidence wouldn't have done you no good, miss. Nor will the rest of the money. You can't spend it, not anywhere on this island.'

'I told you I don't *have* the damned money! Are you calling me a liar?'

'A liar and a thief, I believe, are the words Mr Maitland used.'

It was the last straw. I turned and left the room and ran back up to Mama and Esther. A moment later I heard the officer walk out the front door, and from the window I saw him enter Maitland's carriage. I felt nauseated by the ordeal. I was too upset to talk rationally or even to think. I sunk on to the bed and told them what had happened. It felt as though I were relating a nightmare—that soon I'd wake up and it would be only a bad dream. Mama and Esther drew a coverlet over me, as I was trembling like a leaf, and left. I lay stretched out on the bed to recuperate. I couldn't have felt more battered if a stagecoach and four horses had run over me.

What evil spirit possessed this house? Since the first moment I had set foot in it there had been nothing but trouble and questions that had no answers. Where was the money? Why had Graham given five hundred pounds to K. Norman, and where was K. Norman? What was my fiance doing with a miniature of a ravishingly beautiful young woman under his pillow? Esther had attached a knock-kneed badger who was as close to a moonling as made no difference, and Mama a drunken old reprobate. And compared to myself, they had done well. At least their gentlemen didn't hide their faults. They didn't pretend to love them then call in the police.

Coming to London had been a very bad idea. I would turn the sale of the house over to a real estate agent and take the family home before we ended up in prison. Tomorrow Eliot was bringing the carriage. I found I no longer wanted it, nor any other memento of dear, unfaithful Graham. Who *could* she be, that smiling woman? I'd have Eliot take the carriage back to the stable to be sold, and we would bolt back to Bath.

The hard decision had been taken, and what had delayed it for so long? As if I didn't know! I had countenanced the folly of the family because I was involved in a worse folly myself—the folly of thinking Desmond could possibly love me, when all he was doing was using me. He had arranged the card game 'to get a sample of my blunt,' as the officer so genteelly put it. He had told me the bills were unmarked in hopes that I would feel free to use them. He had baited his trap, and though I was innocent, I was caught in it.

Once the decision to return home was made, I began to settle down to more rational thought. Where had the pound banknote come from, the one with the little cut on the side? I had won it at cards, but was it Yootha or Mr Stone who had given it to me? Mr Stone, wasn't it? Yes, Yootha had lost only a shilling. I sat bolt upright, thinking furiously. Then it was Mr Stone who had the money, obviously! And this very night we were engaged to go to the theater with a drunken thief with whom Mama was fast falling in love.

I jumped up and ran to the saloon to inform her of my discovery. She was still too infatuated to accept it. 'You're a hard judge, Belle,' she said mildly. 'If the Mint damaged one lot of bills, they probably damaged hundreds—thousands.'

'But these were new old bills,' I argued, and had to explain my paradoxical statement till she understood it.

'Gracious, that doesn't mean Mr Stone stole the money. He might have gotten it anywhere. At the bank, or from a friend. Why, he plays cards with everyone, even the prince himself. My, you don't think Prinny . . .' Her hand flew to her lips. 'No, it must be someone else.'

'I'm going to send a note around to Mr Duke cancelling the engagement tonight.'

Esther first howled, then burst into noisy tears, and finally fell at my feet, grabbing my skirts and begging. It would take a heart of steel to deny her, and mine was only stone. She was already crestfallen to be leaving London so soon; missing her one and only chance to see a play—well, it was too much. There were the beautiful new gowns to be considered as well. We were all vain enough to want to wear them. We finally arranged that I would write to Mr Duke informing him that we did not wish to be of the same party as Mr Maitland. I doubted Maitland would have the nerve to keep the engagement, but there must be no possibility of it. If Mr Duke were agreeable to making other arrangements, we would condescend to accompany him, and even that old thief, Stone.

'But you must not quiz him about the money, Belle,' Mama bargained. I agreed, but meant to hazard a few questions all the same.

Hotchkiss delivered the note, and we all sat on tenterhooks awaiting his return. Would Mr Duke be at home? Would he find a replacement for Mr Maitland, or at least agree to remove him, who was an older friend than we, after all, from the party? Esther was nearly climbing the walls by the time Hotchkiss got back. Mr Duke was with him, full of apologies and jumbled explanations. In his shock, he forgot to be quite as terrified of me as formerly and was only ludicrously polite instead.

'A million apologies, Miss Haley! I cannot think what possessed Des, for in the usual way he is the best of good fellows, I promise you. Something must have gotten his dander up, and he never saying a word to me!'

'For that, at least, I am grateful,' I assured him. 'It would be the outside of enough if he announced his unfounded suspicions to the world!'

'By Jove, he never would. Close as an oyster, and an excellent fine chap. Only, of course, he always was a bit of a hothead. I don't know how I shall tell him he cannot come with us tonight, when he was looking forward to it so.'

'He cannot be thinking of coming!' Esther gasped, afraid that she would lose her treat yet.

'No, no, of course not,' Duke said swiftly, then went on to reveal the reverse. 'I shall talk him out of it somehow, never fear. I'll tell him—why, I shall tell him Miss Haley don't care for his company. That ought to do it,' he said, looking timidly at me.

'That is exactly what I would like you to tell him, Duke,' I said approvingly.

Still, there was much talk and much wine taken before the slow creature finally got pen to paper and wrote the note, for he hesitated to inform his friend in person. He sent his groom off with the message and stayed with us till an answer was received. Actually, two letters were delivered, one to me, and it was thick enough to rouse my curiosity. With a great show of anger I ripped the thing in many pieces and threw it on the fire without opening it while Duke read his letter.

'He might have had some explanation, Belle,' Mama mentioned.

'I am not interested in Mr Maitland's explanations, Mama,' I said firmly, counting on Duke to tell him so.

'By Jove,' Duke said, staring at my behavior.

'Will you find me another escort, Duke, or am I to ride bobbin with all you loving couples?' I inquired.

'I don't think I know anyone who would dare . . . That is to say, at the last minute, you know . . . Perhaps Uncle Charles could find someone.'

'Try Two Legs Thomson,' I suggested airily and in jest.

Later that evening, when we had made our toilettes and admired one another's gowns and finally greeted the gentlemen in our saloon, it was indeed Two Legs Thomson who held his arm out to me, and it was to Two Legs Thomson's heavy-handed gallantry that I had to listen all evening.

'It was kind of you to invite me, ma'am,' he began. 'You quite turned my head with the honor. "Get me Two Legs Thomson," you said, quick as blinking, when young Duke asked who you would have.'

I glared at Duke. He jiggled in behind Esther and smiled—or I think that frightened look was supposed to have been a smile, at any rate. Already Two Legs had my hands in his. Before he took the notion that I had fallen in love with him, I had to quench his ardor. 'The thing is, I don't know any gentlemen in London. None at all, other than you,' I explained.

He winked his eyes, ducked his head, and whispered, 'You won't need to know any others. I can handle you all by myself, miss.'

I wrenched my hands free and whisked away to the sofa, which had room only for one. Another mistake. It gave him an excuse to squeeze in uncomfortably close to me. I could smell the spirits on his breath, feel the heat from his bulky body, and I felt imprisoned. All my time was occupied restraining Thomson, which prevented my learning a thing from Stone about where he had gotten that banknote. It was going to be a fitting night to cap a disastrous day.

To escape the sofa and Two Legs, I suggested we depart for the theater a good half hour earlier than necessary, which left us sitting in a nearly empty building, waiting for the audience to join us. My little consolation was that Esther enjoyed it. She made a shameless exhibition of herself, using her fan like an accomplished flirt and using Duke's opera glasses to spy out handsome gentlemen and well-gowned ladies, every one of whom was brought first to Mama's attention, then to mine. More than one hedgebird whose only claim to gentility was the jacket on his back undertook to set up a flirtation with Esther, and she managed to indulge them all. She was smiling and nodding around the hall like a regular coquette.

Only the haziest memories of what occurred onstage remain with me. It was a wildly active romantic farce of some sort that kept the audience in peals of laughter. At the intermission some of Esther's conquests invaded our box, making it impossible for me to get out and stretch my legs, for I didn't dare to leave Esther untended while Mama and Mr Stone left for a glass of wine.

What got me through the evening was knowing that in a few hours it would be over and we could escape back to Elm Street. I would lie down and forget this hideous interval. I would put from my mind Two Legs's winey breath in my face, his foraging hands, which constantly required removal from my waist, my hip, my hands. I would forget his slanderous comments on the audience and the miserable feeling that I had somehow descended for an evening in hell. The noise and din and lights would fade to blissful dark silence.

During the last act of the play I became aware of a gentleman across the hall who was apparently under the impression that the performance was in our box. He had his glasses trained on us unwaveringly. Another conquest for Esther, I thought, and I was about to turn away when he lowered his glasses and I saw that it was Desmond Maitland.

It took all my self-control to remain seated. My instinct was to jump up, fly across the hall, and beat him, but I did the polite thing and turned away. Not once more that evening did my eyes go a fraction of an inch left of center stage. I even quelled the urge to see who was with him, for he was in a full box, and I was a little curious to examine his companion. She was a young, pretty woman with dark hair and a red gown. White shoulders rose above the gown, and she appeared to be staring every bit as hard as Maitland.

When the play was over the ordeal ought to have been at an end; but no, Mr Stone had arranged a dinner for us at the Pulteney Hotel. I began talking this down, but Mama got me aside and said, 'They will expect to come home with us for a bite to eat if we don't go, Belle. This is the easier way—we can leave them at the door.'

I girded my courage for another hour of forced gaiety and noise. Half the theaters in

178

town emptied into the hotel after the show. The place was even more crowded and noisy than the Haymarket, but we were soon ensconced in a private parlor. The diversion of having a full plate in front of him gave Two Legs something else to do with his hands besides maul me. I ate a little and drank two glasses of wine, which improved my mood. It allowed me to imagine some humor in the affair. I must have become a little bosky, for in fact our night had more in common with vulgar melodrama than with comedy.

The elder gentlemen drank a deal of wine, Duke rather less. He stated two or three times that what we had seen was what he would call a play. When it was time to go home the two carriages were brought around. I had been unhappy to leave Mama and Mr Stone alone for the trip to the theater but felt she was an uncertain chaperon for Esther. With Mr Stone three sheets to the wind, I determined I would not abandon Mama to him. Yet to leave Esther, a young girl, alone with Duke was worse. I solved the dilemma by admitting to Duke that I disliked his uncle's condition and charging him most severely with getting both Mama and Esther home safely.

'You arranged the party. It is for you to see that no harm comes to the ladies,' I pointed out.

'Daresay I can handle Uncle Charles. He don't turn rusty when he's disguised. Two Legs might. This breaking up will leave you alone with Two Legs,' he pointed out.

'There are two carriages, and we cannot all crowd into one. I can handle Two Legs.'

'I daresay you can,' he admitted.

My proud boast was soon put to the test. The sly old gaffer gave his driver some secret direction to drive us not home to Elm Street but to Hyde Park. In the dark of night, and lacking much familiarity with London, I didn't realize we were going the wrong direction. I was pretty busy finding excuses to move from one banquette to the other to escape Two Legs's advances. Not till the driver actually pulled into the shadowed drive of the park did I discover his stunt, and by then I had more than an inkling why he had chosen this dark, isolated spot. Even before his arm slid around my waist and pulled me along the seat, I knew what he was up to.

'Behave yourself, Two Legs!' I exclaimed, and pushed him away.

'I like a lively lass,' he said, laughing, and attacked me. His wine-soaked lips groped for mine. It was the most disgusting thing you can imagine, to have a drunken old lecher chasing you around a carriage. He was uninsultable. All my angry chiding was taken for playful encouragement.

'Never you mind, missie. Two Legs you wanted, and Two Legs you shall have. I've had my eye on you before. I was a little shy to speak up, but you showed me the way. Aye, it was thoughtful of you to get rid of the others. I couldn't have done better myself.'

'I shall show you the way out of this carriage if you don't sit back and behave yourself, sir!' I informed him.

'Nay, we'd both prefer the comfort and privacy of the coach,' he rallied. 'I'm too old for performing outdoors.'

There was a new, frightening tone creeping into his voice. His hands, too, grew bolder at every attack. There was no reasoning with him. A rising panic invaded me. I would have to escape—to jump out of the carriage and lose myself in the shadows of the park. When the horses slowed down at a curve I already had my hand on the door handle. I threw it open and rolled out on the ground. Thomson's carriage drew to a halt a few yards farther on. Two Legs got out, and I struggled to my feet to run. He moved very swiftly for an old man, whereas I was hampered by long skirts and high-heeled slippers.

The park was deserted at half past midnight. The air was cold, and the only illumination was a crescent moon, half concealed by clouds. Trees in the park rose up like black shadows in the still, gray silence. The only sounds were the wind in the trees, the soft thud of our feet hitting earth, and our gasping for air as we pelted along. I thought of abandoning the road, running into the bushes

181

and trees, but I was afraid the footing would be even worse there; besides, I was just a little afraid of becoming thoroughly lost. Thomson wasn't gaining much on me, but the thudding feet were drawing insensibly closer, and I couldn't run much longer. Just when it began to seem he might overtake me, I saw a hope of rescue that gave me a last burst of energy.

A pair of carriage lights appeared in the distance, coming toward us. Not a moment too soon; my side was cramped and my breaths were hardly strong enough to fill my lungs. I staggered into the path of the oncoming carriage and waved my arms wildly. The driver saw me and yanked the horses to a halt. The welcome jingle of the harness and his hearty 'Whoaa!' were music to my ears. Immediately the door opened and a gentleman got out. With the last of my breath I wobbled toward him as he hastened forward to meet me. When we were about three paces apart, I recognized my savior as Desmond Maitland.

CHAPTER ELEVEN

If there was a fate worse than being caught by Two Legs Thomson, it was being rescued by the abominable creature who stood before me. I tried to revile him, but my breath was gone. I just slumped, panting, and was caught in his arms before I quite hit the ground. A hundred jumbled thoughts and sounds and sights vied for attention in the next minute. I remember Maitland shaking me and demanding to know what had happened, was I hurt, and such things. His face was a white mask of anger glowing in the moonlight. When he had determined I still had some life in me, I was passed from his arms to the driver's. Maitland took off after Two Legs and knocked him down with one smashing blow to the jaw. I don't know which sound was uglier—that of his fist hitting flesh or that of the accompanying curse—but both struck me as eminently suitable. Maitland returned and bundled me into the carriage. His angry mask had petrified into something resembling rock.

There were no warm bricks this time, but my feet burned from flying along the stony path. Maitland threw the fur rug over me, and I just as quickly shucked it off. My deep breaths reverberated in the small closed space. They were the only sound till Maitland drew a bottle of wine from the side pocket, uncorked it, and handed it to me without a glass.

Then I realized my throat was parched, and I lifted the bottle to drink directly from it. My arms were trembling, and my gasping for breath caused a gulping, unladylike sound. I drank deeply, then handed the bottle back to Mr Maitland. Should I thank him, I wondered, or should I follow my heart and leave without

183

a word?

While I pondered this decision his voice cut like a knife into the dark silence. 'I hope you're satisfied!'

I had been anticipating various reactions from him—an apology, sympathy—but certainly not this cold, vehement anger. Coming on top of a long, extremely vexing night, it was enough to annihilate common sense. 'No, I'm far from satisfied! I'd as lief have been caught by Thomson as rescued by you!' On this brave speech I reached for the door handle.

His hand shot out and grabbed mine in a painful grip. I didn't hesitate to use my nails to discourage him. When he pulled back in surprise I opened the door and jumped out. I wasn't sure whether I had jumped from the frying pan into the fire or the reverse, but the park looked even darker than before, and I stood a moment before striking off down the road, away from Thomson. Though I would never in a million years have admitted it, I was half relieved when the door opened and he came after me. I hastened my steps along till he was required to run to catch me. He didn't try to stop me or say anything but just walked along a step behind me, like a prince consort. I heard the carriage turn around and come lumbering after us.

We came to a turning in the road, and I had to stop to get my bearings. Maitland stopped as well, waiting. I turned left, and his hand fell on my arm. 'You're headed to Belgrave Square. Elm Street is this way,' he said.

'Thank you, and now that I know the way, it won't be necessary for you to accompany me.'

'Consider me a shadow.'

I turned and headed toward Elm Street. I held my head high, which gave me no view at all of the road or of the large rock in my path. I was walking hard and fast and struck it with enough force to give me a very real fear that I had broken my toe. I couldn't suppress one little yelp of pain. I took another step, however, and winced. By then it was clear that I wasn't going to walk home.

Maitland raised his arm to have the carriage draw up, and he held the door. I was so frustrated I wanted to kick him—or the carriage—but my throbbing toe warned me against such a course. I got in and sat stiff as a ramrod while Maitland took a seat beside me, and the carriage rumbled into motion. My ignominious situation improved his humor. His voice was hardly more than furious when he asked, 'Just what in God's name did you think you were doing?'

'I was going home after the worst evening—and day!—of my life.'

His reply had the force of a whip lashing the air. 'Whose fault is that? You wouldn't have been attacked by that old pervert if you hadn't climbed into a carriage alone with him. There may be some excuse for Esther's behaving like a lightskirt—she at least is young and inexperienced. You're plenty old enough to know better. Your day, *and mine,* would have been less hideous if you'd told me the truth about the money.'

Just when I thought I hadn't an ounce of fight left in me I was suddenly alive again and burning as brightly as a gas lamp. 'Thank you for calling me a liar—and a thief! I know money holds a paramount position in your scale of values, but it matters less to me. I am sorry you were unable to find your money. No doubt it's a grievance to you that you aren't able to pocket the five thousand belonging to Mr Pelty, but you are mistaken, as you must surely know by now, to think I have it. We at Elm Street were very much amused by your little comedy—your game of cards to see the color of our blunt, and your assuring us the bills were unmarked so we would feel free to spend them. Unfortunately for you, we had only the one cut bill. Perhaps you could take the scissors to some of your other friends' money and have the law down on them instead.' My rant done, I turned my head aside and looked out the window at the darkness.

He lunged forward, grabbed my chin, and forcibly turned my head back to face him. 'What was I to think? You had the banknote!'

I wrenched his hand away and threw it back at him. 'Don't touch me again. You thought I

186

had the lot long before that, or you wouldn't have put us to the test! How dare you come into our home like a friend and treat us so shabbily!'

'You just accused *me* of trying to bilk Pelty!'

'I'd accuse you of murdering Graham if I could! I wouldn't put it a bit past you.'

'Belle, I wasn't trying to con you. I admit I first struck up an acquaintance with that in mind, but I had dismissed you as the culprit days ago. I did it only to set Pelty's mind at rest. He's been nattering at me that "Miss Haley has to know something," and I did it to prove to him you were innocent. You could have knocked me over with a breath when I looked at that banknote and saw the cut. You gave Eliot Sutton that letter authorizing him to get the carriage. It was possible the money was there.'

'Eliot hasn't even gotten it yet!'

'His groom could have. I tell you that pound came from the money that disappeared. Where did you get it?'

'Are you sure you'd believe the word of a *liar,* Mr Maitland?'

'I'm not responsible for what I might have said to Roy after you gave me that banknote. I felt betrayed. He told me you tried to burn the bill—does that sound like innocence to you?'

'He's lucky it wasn't him I chucked into the grate. I only did it in a fit of temper.'

'A fit of temper isn't going to get us very

far,' he said impatiently.

'At least it'll get me home. I'm sorry I ever came up to London. But maybe it did me some good after all. I wasn't completely convinced there was a devil; now I know that London's full of them.'

'You've managed to entangle your halo in more than one set of horns. What was Thomson up to in the carriage that you felt required to bolt?'

'Just what you think.'

'You had some notion how he would behave in private. His hands were all over you at the play. Why did you drive home with him?'

'Because I couldn't leave Mama or Esther alone with those jackanapes! I couldn't be with *both* of them. Are you suggesting I *wanted . . .*' My voice broke in indignation, and I felt tears scald my eyes. I blinked them away, only to hear a miserable hiccuping sound erupt from my throat. It was the aftermath of my long ordeal, for I am not a watering pot.

Maitland used it as an excuse to grab my hands. 'Are you sure you're all right? I'll go back and knock that bleater's tooth down his throat.'

'I'm fine. Pass that wine, will you, please? I think I'm getting the hiccups,' I said, hoping to pass it off in that manner. He handed me the bottle and I took a short sip.

'You could have accepted my escort. I only went to the concert to see you, to try to find a chance to talk to you. It's lucky I followed Thomson's carriage—I thought I might catch you at your door.'

'That's not a very flattering remark on your lady friend's company. If lady is the correct term for a woman who appears in public half-dressed.'

'I was with my sister,' he said, his voice thinning.

'Pardon me. In that case, I admired her skirt enormously.'

'This isn't Bath. Fashion is more daring in London. We may seem fast to you, but I've never caused you to leave the carriage, at least.'

'I've already left it once tonight, and I'd leave it this minute if my toe weren't aching like a bad tooth.'

We continued a moment in silence. As we drove east on Piccadilly he took the wine and set it aside. The gas lamps in this quarter made it easier to see in the carriage. I noticed he had crossed his arms and leaned back at his ease to enjoy the squabble. 'Did you get my letter?'

'Yes.'

'Well, now that you've had a chance to calm down, will you do it?'

'Do what?'

'What I asked.'

'I didn't say I *read* the letter. I threw it in the grate.'

His lips moved unsteadily. 'I must be wary

of standing too close to that grate. I see it serves as your dustbin for unwanted objects.'

'Don't worry. You'll never be anywhere near it, unless your aunt buys the house. Not that I believe for a minute you even have an aunt.'

'I have five.'

'That doesn't make you a member of the human race.'

'You lack certain human qualities yourself, Belle. If you were a normal woman, you'd be curious to know what was in that letter.'

I was willing to listen but refused to ask. After another moment's silence he gave in and told me. 'You've convinced me you don't have the money. I believe you. I just want you to tell me one thing. Where did you get that banknote?'

'Why should I bring Officer Roy down on the head of a friend?'

'Eliot?'

'Certainly not.'

'Yootha?'

'No.'

'It can't be Two Legs. You'd have the law on him fast enough.'

'I wish I could say it was him, but it wasn't.'

'And it wasn't Duke . . . Stone!' he exclaimed triumphantly.

'Yes, it was Stone. I meant to quiz him tonight and see if I could learn anything, but I was too busy.'

'I noticed at the play. You must have been

even busier in the carriage. And the park is hardly safe at night, either.'

'Very true. I met you there, didn't I?'

He ventured a rallying smile. 'Aren't you glad you did? I don't expect thanks for rescuing you, but I hardly expected verbal abuse after my flowery letter of apology, which, of course, you didn't bother to read. Since you didn't read it, I shall apologize in person now. Belle, I'm damnably sorry. If I'd had the least notion how things would turn out, I wouldn't have gotten that warrant. It was the unconsidered act of a moment's temper, when I thought you were playing me for a dupe. You know how you felt when I landed in —I saw that awful, disbelieving look on your face. That's how I felt when I saw the banknote. I thought you and Eliot were working together—maybe in tandem with Mrs Mailer, whom you call "*Aunt* Yootha," as though you were all one happy family. I wasn't rational; I just wanted to hurt and humiliate you. Even then, I had no notion of letting it go to court. I hope you can believe that and understand how I felt.'

'Despite my best intentions of being intransigent, I *do* understand. At some future date, after my toe stops throbbing like a drum, I'm sure I shall forgive, too. Please don't ask it of me tonight. Between the picture and the search warrant and Four Hands Thomson, I'm afraid . . .'

I felt his hands grabbing mine, not with any amorous intent, but in surprise. 'What picture?' he asked swiftly.

I was distressed at what had slipped out and tried to brush it aside, but he persisted shamelessly. 'Just a little ivory miniature I found in the house.'

'The picture of the blonde under Graham's pillow?' he asked.

So he had seen it in his searches. My full shame was known by him all along—that Graham had served me false—and I, like an idiot, had been hailing him as a paragon.

'There's no reason to think it means anything, Belle,' he consoled me. 'She's probably a favorite niece or cousin.'

I grasped at this slender straw for appearance's sake. Though Graham had never favored one particular niece or cousin over another, I knew that he had several. 'Of course that must be it, but it gave me a bit of a surprise.'

Desmond regaled me with imaginary tales of favorite female relatives whose likenesses encumbered his bedroom, and I, with equal civility, did not call him liar but only asked, 'Are you sure you have room for a bed with all those pictures cluttering up the place, Desmond?'

He turned a sparkling eye on me. 'Definitely. I consider a bed one of life's greatest necessities—and pleasures, if one has the proper companion.'

'In your case, that would mean a female, I presume?'

'A female? I don't accept just any indefinite article in my bed. She must be *the* female of my choice.'

By the time we reached Elm Street all our anger and mistrust had evaporated. I had accidentally called him Desmond once, and it seemed artificial to return to Mr Maitland after that.

'I'll get on to Stone tomorrow,' he said when the carriage drew to a stop. 'I'll have Grant take a look around his place. I have a few other ideas as well.'

'What kind of ideas?'

'I plan to return to the scene of the crime— not your place but where the trade was made—and follow Graham's route home. We originally thought he might have dropped the bundle off at K. Norman's flat, you recall. He didn't, but I may be struck with some other inspiration as I drive along.'

'If you ask me very nicely, I might go with you,' I offered.

'Then I shan't ask you nicely. You wouldn't enjoy it.'

My extraordinary condescension in offering was rejected out of hand. It was enough to return me to bad humor and make me realize how thoroughly despicable Desmond Maitland was.

'Then I shall have Eliot take me. He's dropping by tomorrow,' I said, but I was very careful not to make it sound spiteful.

'That will teach me a lesson! I can be led, Belle, but not by childish threats.'

'*Do* tell me the secret, in case I ever want to lead you anywhere. Coventry comes to mind.'

'Most ladies find *this* the best way,' he said, and swept me into his arms.

For the second time that night I was victimized by a person who considered himself a gentleman. Mr Maitland had been drinking wine, like Mr Thomson. He was every bit as persistent, yet the overall experience was entirely dissimilar. His young lips burned hot, and mine responded, against my better judgment. The heat radiated through me and around us, firing spirit and imagination with emotions never felt before. As a clergyman's daughter, I made token recognition that this must be wrong, yet it felt absolutely right and natural and inevitable. And rapturously ecstatic.

My voice, when at last I was free to speak, was a trembling whisper. 'I really must go now.'

'Am I tarnishing your halo, darling?' he teased. His dark eyes caught a light from the street lamps and reflected it just before his head descended again. I turned my halo to escape further tarnishing and discovered a spot more sensitive than the lips. A warm

194

breath penetrated my ear as his lips nibbled at the lobe. Those same breaths entered my body, causing tremendous chaos as they surged to my brain and billowed through the bloodstream to cause havoc in my breast.

I moved again, but his arms prevented any drastic physical estrangement between us. His lips nibbled at my jaw and brushed down my neck to the hollow of my throat, and I could feel my heart pulse at a fast beat. The whole world seemed to be turning faster, at a dizzying speed. His cheek felt warm against my breast, and his hair was as rich and soft as merino under my fingers.

Then he raised his head and gazed at me. With a perfectly serious face he asked, 'May I take it you and I are no longer sworn enemies, Miss Haley?'

'I hardly ever permit sworn enemies to compromise me, Mr Maitland.'

A smile broke. 'Compromise? I would hardly say we had gone so far as all that! An Esther might be compromised by a kiss, but surely a woman who has been engaged may be allowed a little more latitude in her dealings.'

'In London, perhaps. In Bath, I assure you, this engaged lady was never so well handled as she has been this night.'

He seemed surprised; taken aback is hardly too strong to describe the startled face he wore. 'I'm afraid I got carried away. Next time I shall try to behave as properly as the Bath

195

gentlemen.'

'Comparisons are odious, Des. Just try to believe I am not a liar and a thief. That will do for a start.'

'Let us both try to develop some trust. I won't believe you want to steal the money if you promise to believe *I'm* not out to bilk Pelty. That stung, my sweet!'

'Good! Now you know how I felt.'

'Angels are subject to revenge, are they?' he asked, and chucked my chin. 'My reading of theology is outdated. Your mama will think you one of the fallen angels if you go in looking like this.'

I thought I must be showing the afterglow of our embraces, but when he took out his handkerchief and wiped a smudge of dust from my cheek I realized he had referred to my tumble in the dust.

'I see the lights are on, so they made it safely home. They'll be worried about me. I must go.'

'Dare I present myself at your door tomorrow?'

'I'll pave the way.'

We got out and Desmond walked me to the door. 'I'm really very sorry for all the trouble I've caused you, Belle. One day we'll look back and laugh at it, eh?' This intimation of a shared future brought a smile to my face. 'I see you can smile already.'

'I'm too tired to frown or scold.'

'Good, such opportunities can't be wasted.' I received another crushing kiss and went in, still hot from lovemaking, to deliver a halfhearted scold to Esther and Mama. But I could not be too severe with them, for they were so very concerned about my safety and the destruction of my new bronze gown. It was a shambles, but not nearly so bad as my coiffure and dirty face—and, of course, my toe, which was rapidly turning a nasty livid shade. I made much of Desmond's heroic behavior in order to pave the way for his return.

'Since he's back in your good books, it's a pity you looked so horrid,' Esther pointed out.

'Some people don't judge by looks, Esther,' I said grandly. 'You, for instance, don't seem to care a groat that Mr Duke is an ankle biter. I *do* admire your being able to overlook his appearance. It seems Des doesn't mind my looking like a beggar, either.'

She chose to take this as a compliment on her character, and we all retired happily.

CHAPTER TWELVE

The tyrant was in top form next morning to trim her brood into line. Mama was subjected to a scold for not having quizzed Mr Stone about the banknote.

'I did not want to hurt his feelings, Belle. I am more convinced than ever that he had nothing to do with it. It is that Maitland fellow who has turned your head again, even after the way he treated us.'

'He treated *me* very well, Mama. If it were not for him, I wouldn't be here with you today but would be in some home for seduced and abandoned women,' I reminded her. 'Where Esther will end up if she continues carrying on as she did last night.'

Esther paid no heed. She was off in the clouds remembering the glory of Haymarket, or perhaps the grandeur of Mr Duke's five feet and four inches of chubbiness. After my scold, I had one piece of good news for them.

'I have decided to hire a team for Graham's carriage for the remainder of our short stay.'

'Do you think it worthwhile for only a day?' Mama asked.

'We may end up staying a little longer, since the house is still unsold. As you said, why pay a real estate agent two hundred and fifty guineas when we don't have to? Eliot is bringing the carriage around today, using his own team till he hires me a pair.'

Eliot, while acceptable, had not found any great degree of favor with Mama and Esther. They went out to inspect the carriage, but when he offered us all a drive to test its springs, they declined.

'I shall be back within half an hour,' I told

them, lest they had any ideas of sending off notes to Messrs. Stone and Duke.

The privacy with Eliot was welcome, as I had a few questions to put to him. First in importance was the matter of the banknote given to me by Stone. Omitting the incident of the search warrant, I told him Mr Maitland's opinion of that note. 'You know Stone better than we do, Eliot. Do you think it possible he was involved in that business?'

'I hardly know him that well. I run into him occasionally at Aunt Yootha's place. He doesn't cheat at cards, and he's well enough to grass that he wouldn't have to steal, but whether he did it for a lark—no, I hardly think so. You know my opinion as to who is responsible for the theft,' he added. 'Mr Maitland rigged the whole thing himself to do Pelty out of his five thousand. He's probably pulled off this stunt a dozen times. Did you notice this cut in the banknote?'

'No, but I really don't think Mr Maitland would be looking so hard for the money if he had had it all the time,' I pointed out.

'What better way to convince the world he's innocent?'

'If one of the Lloyd's agents is responsible, it is surely Mr Pelty. *He* is the one who actually handled the transaction. Mr Maitland was out of town that night.'

'That's exactly what makes me suspect him. Mind you, it could be Pelty. He's only a name to me.'

Our conversation was punctuated with comments about the comfort of the carriage and about the country wedding Eliot had attended. The next item pertaining to the case was the miniature I carried in my reticule. I decided to show it to him, and I asked if he recognized the girl.

His fingers made a spontaneous grab for it. 'Where did you get this?' he asked sharply.

'I found it in Graham's room. You obviously recognize her. Who is she?'

He took a few seconds to consider before replying, but when he spoke it sounded like the truth. 'It's a woman Graham was seeing before he met you. I don't know her name, but he used to take her out to an occasional play or dinner.'

'Perhaps Yootha will recognize her.'

'I said a woman, not a lady.' He turned a sober mien toward me. 'Belle, let sleeping dogs lie.'

'I wouldn't call her a dog! She has a kittenish prettiness about her. What kind of a woman is she?'

'The kind of woman a young, lonesome bachelor takes up with. That's Graham's past—distant past. Don't sully your memories of him by harping on it. She meant nothing to him once he met you. Please give me the thing and forget you ever saw it.'

My answer was to put it in my purse and

snap the fastener. Graham wouldn't have had it under his pillow if she meant nothing to him. 'You are being extremely unhelpful, Eliot. Your reticence only makes me more curious than ever. I mean to discover who the girl is.'

He turned sulky. 'What about the carriage? Will you keep it or put it up for sale?'

'I shall keep it, by all means, and hire a team of job horses. Will you handle that for me?'

'You could get more than a hundred guineas for the rig,' he tempted.

'Yes, and I could pay twice that for a new one. Ours at home is a disgrace. I shall keep it.'

'Have you had any offers on the house?'

'No serious offers.'

'Why don't you put it with an agent?'

'Because I'm all skint. I don't want to pay the commission.'

'I'll be happy to act as your agent without a fee. Truly, I shouldn't mind at all.'

'You sound mighty eager to be rid of us, Eliot!' I chided playfully.

'Rid of you! Belle, how can you say such a thing? I am only thinking of your best interests. Why, the whole family has been deriding London since the moment you arrived. I thought you were eager to go home, but if you plan to make a longer stay of it, we must organize some entertainment for you.'

I found Mr Maitland much more entertaining than Eliot and didn't encourage this line. After a quarter of an hour, the carriage was turned around and we went home. I invited him in for wine, but he had an appointment and couldn't accept. He promised to bring a team around for my inspection in the very near future, and he left.

After I had removed my bonnet and pelisse, I put my three mysterious clues on the bed and sat looking at them. A painting of a woman, a key to an unknown door, and the address book bearing the name K. Norman of Fleury Lane. The three items lying there together fell into place so easily I could only stare at my own stupidity in not assembling them mentally before now. The girl was K. Norman, and the key was the key to her flat—and I didn't overlook that Graham had still had the key on his key ring when he was killed.

I was overcome with morbid curiosity. What kind of a man had I been engaged to? I even found myself wondering if Graham had ever intended to return the case of money to its rightful owner. And if he had been in love with K. Norman, why had he proposed marriage to me? He was no fortune hunter—if he had been, he would have looked beyond my pittance. No, he had loved K. Norman, but had he loved me? K. Norman was not a lady, according to Eliot. Had Graham been tempted to marry her anyway, and had he taken the step of allying himself with me to prevent such a social disaster? After my amorous experiences with Des, I realized Graham's lovemaking had been extremely perfunctory. Any woman but a greenhorn would have realized it, but to me it had been a magnificent affair. How many handkerchiefs had I wet with my salty tears?

My aim now was to go and visit K. Norman. I mentally christened her Kitty, to match her face. Both Eliot and Des had said K Norman no longer lived in Fleury Lane, but they had only wanted to save me the embarrassment of learning about her. That was why Des had so adamantly refused to take me there. It wasn't the neighborhood, close to Long Acre, but the occupant of Fleury Lane, 2B. I didn't care a fig that Eliot knew, but it stung to think Des knew I had never been loved.

I was on thorns to see Kitty but didn't want Mama to learn a thing about her. On the other hand, I could not go alone. Esther? It wouldn't do that flirt any harm to see how she might end up if she didn't mend her coquettish ways. In the end, I decided to take only Hotchkiss with me and to go as soon as Eliot got me a team.

This happened more quickly than I expected. That same afternoon the pair was brought around, but Eliot did not accompany them. He had sent his groom instead, but I packed him off for privacy's sake.

'Come back in an hour and remove the carriage. Where is it to be stabled?'

'With Mr Eliot's, for the time being,' the groom said. He scampered away quite happily.

Unfortunately, Esther took it into her head to accompany me, and I had uphill work convincing her that I was only going out to pick up some books at the circulating library. That finally subdued her interest. Books were a plague to her, and a library under quarantine.

Hotchkiss was as nervous as a deb on his maiden journey into the heavy traffic of London. We stopped to buy a map at a news stall and pored over it together, searching out Fleury Lane. It wasn't that far away, but the streets resembled a patchwork quilt, and Hotchkiss got lost a dozen times. The better part of an hour had passed before he discovered the little road, really no more than a back alley bearing a sign, 'Fleury Lane.' It was entirely disreputable. How was it possible Graham had sought out a woman in this neighborhood—or, worse, established his mistress here?

The roadway was littered with the debris of humanity: papers blowing in the wind, an old abandoned boot, broken wine bottles, and a skinny brindled cat. Hotchkiss drove at a slow pace to allow me to scan the house numbers. There it was, No. 2, halfway down the lane—a shabby old stone building three stories high with a faded blue door bearing no knocker. I was frightened to enter the place alone and afraid to leave the carriage untended.

'If I'm not back in five minutes, Hotchkiss, come to my rescue,' I ordered.

I had confessed the purpose of the visit to him, and he had agreed to accompany me only when I had threatened to go alone in a hackney. 'You're mad as a hatter!' he warned, and he handed me a little paring knife from Ettie's kitchen. I put it in my pocket and marched bravely to the blue door. My first knock brought no answer. My second knock was louder, and a dissolute-looking old hag in a mobcap came limping to answer.

'I'm looking for K. Norman, at 2B.'

'Upstairs,' she growled, and returned to her own lair.

The staircase was narrow, steep, and dirty. Even the air was foul, reeking of boiled cabbage and squalor. I lifted my skirts, avoided any contact with the banister, and went up. At the top of the landing I saw rows of doors down either side of a hallway. The first on my left said 2B. I tapped sharply on the door and held my breath.

There was no answer, but I heard light footsteps and tapped again.

'Who is it?' a soft voice called.

'It is a friend, to see K. Norman.'

'Oh, a lady! I—I suppose that would be all right.'

Within two seconds the door opened inward and I finally beheld K. Norman in the flesh.

She seemed like a delicate flower blooming amid the garbage of Fleury Lane. She was a perfectly exquisite little thing, even prettier than her picture. Her gown was old and frayed, but clean and once fashionable. I wondered if Graham had given it to her. While I stared at her she narrowed her incomparable eyes and examined my bonnet and gown. The vision of loveliness opened its lips and emitted an atrocious accent.

'What do you want?'

'I'm looking for Miss Norman.'

'I'm her. Who sent you?'

'May I come in?'

'My gentleman told me not to see anybody.'

I noted that she had replaced Graham. 'I didn't come to harm you. I have something that belongs to you.'

'What is it, then?' she asked suspiciously.

I drew out the ivory miniature and handed it to her. While she examined it I slid in past her and found myself standing in a low, dark hallway, but at its end a brighter living room received the sun. I couldn't see anyone else, and I felt emboldened to walk toward the living room. 'Here, where are you going?' she called, hurrying after me.

'I thought we might have a little chat, Miss Norman.'

'My name's Kate.'

'How lovely.'

She kept looking at the miniature. 'Grame

206

had this painted. You knew Grame?'

'Yes, I knew him.'

A frown creased her brow as she looked again at the miniature. 'Are you Mrs Mailer?' she asked.

Concealing my identity seemed a good idea, and I said, 'Yes, Graham's aunt.'

'I thought you'd be older,' she said doubtfully, but in the end she accepted me. I daresay my twenty-three years seemed old enough to her. She was still not more than eighteen, I figured, and must have been—my God!—younger than Esther when Graham was with her. I felt a deep disgust with him, worse than anything before.

The only emotion I could feel for the girl was pity. I wanted to do something for her, give her some money. We sat down in her little living room, a cozy tidy place. It bore some evidence of Graham's bent for finery. Velvet draperies at the windows contrasted sharply with the bare wood floors and chipped furnishings that graced the modest room. A framed painting of Graham sat on a desk in the corner.

'You are managing all right since Graham's death, Kate? You have found a new protector?'

'I have now,' she answered, and smiled. An enchanting pair of dimples quivered at the corners of her lips. 'My new gent's moving me to the country.'

'Will you like that?'

'I don't mind. And it will be good for Baba.'

'Ah, you have a child!' Another arrow pierced my heart. 'Will your new gentleman marry you?' It was a gauche question. If he had meant to do so, he wouldn't have waited till the child was born.

'Gents don't marry the likes of me. Especially with the baba,' she added bluntly. Child that she was, she had already learned the harsh realities of the world.

'Your gentleman is not the child's father, then?'

My meddling question made her withdraw into herself. She didn't answer but only stared at me. While we sat, a wailing began in another room. Without speaking, she darted up and ran off to the child. She was gone a few minutes; I heard her talking to the baby, and some gurgling sounds in return. She seemed a doting mother, despite her youth.

The gurgling sounds drew nearer, and I knew she was bringing the child for my inspection. I already regretted my visit. It had been nothing but ill-bred curiosity. I would leave immediately—give her whatever money I had in my reticule and flee. Then she was at the door, proudly holding her baby up for my inspection, and any thought of flight vanished. Even if the child's age—somewhere near a year and a half—hadn't told me the name of its father, the characteristic hairline would have done so. I sat mutely staring at a miniature Graham, his noble brow and widow's peak recreated in miniature. The eyes, too—it was a devastating experience. I felt as though I were looking at Graham grown all young and innocent.

Somehow I found my voice. 'He's beautiful. What do you call him?'

'Grame, after his da. Say hello to Aunt Yootha, Baba.'

Then she handed the bundle to me, and I was forced to accept the child. It gave me an excuse to keep my head lowered and conceal my disordered state. Kate waxed quite eloquent over the child's accomplishments, and I found myself nodding and trying to smile and praise, but I hardly knew what I was doing.

'He can walk. Baba, show the nice lady how you can step along.'

The child took two steps and fell on his behind. As she returned him to my lap I inquired for his age.

'A year and a half, ma'am. He can say mama, too, but he's shy. We don't see many strangers.'

She offered tea, but I knew that was beyond me. 'I really must go. I just wanted to—to meet you.'

'Why did you wait so long? Grame said if anything happened to him, you'd come and look after me.'

'When did he say this?' I asked, staring at

her in fascination.

The night he brought the case of money. He said you'd know what was to be done with it, and I mustn't use any of it, not a penny.'

The money! He *did* come here the night—

'Oh, yes, Mrs Mailer. He came pelting to the door and threw it in that closet there.' She pointed to a small door across the room. 'He was frightened half to death. I told him not to go out there again, but after fifteen minutes he was sure the man was gone. He said he'd leave the money in case he was ambushed. I didn't know what to do with it. I tried to find you, Mrs Mailer, but I didn't know where you lived, and when I went to the West End looking for you a lady had the Bow Street Runners called. She said trollops ought to know their place. She didn't know where you lived,' she added forlornly.

I thought my ordeals were bad, but what cruelty this child had been subjected to, and only because she was trying to be honest! 'That is a great pity, Kate. The fact is, Graham didn't give me your address, either.'

She accepted this nonsense humbly. I realized that Yootha had known all about Kate Norman. She had known what a miserable state the girl had ben reduced to when Graham was unexpectedly killed, and she hadn't stirred a finger to help her. She'd have been here fast enough if she'd known about the money! The money was still to be handled.

I felt sure I could convince Des to give Kate a good portion of it as a reward.

'About the money, Kate. As I am here, I shall take it with me.'

She looked puzzled. 'But it's gone now. I gave it to my new gentleman two days ago.'

I sat still, trying to figure out what had happened, who her new gentleman was. 'Mr Stone, you mean?' I inquired.

'Oh, no. It's Mr Maitland. He explained that it was his money all along. He gave me ten pounds' reward and is going to move me and Baba to the country. He told me not to see anybody, but I don't care what he says. I couldn't bar the door to Grame's aunt.'

'Mr Maitland!'

'Yes, the Lloyd's agent. Such a fine gentleman.'

I sat, numb, trying to make heads or tails of her story. Two days ago Des had collected the money. He had had it when he brought Officer Roy to search my house. Eliot was right, then—he was planning to bilk Petty out of his five thousand. Surely she was mistaken! 'A tall, dark-haired gentleman, is he?'

'And handsome. We had such a jolly time out looking for a cottage. Oh, Baba will like the country!' She smiled happily.

'I'm so glad.'

I wanted to leave, but I sat holding the gurgling little pledge of Graham's love and trying to think of a polite way to leave. It was the sound of Hotchkiss's feet on the stairs that finally got me up. Kate grabbed her child and ran to lock the door.

'That will be my groom. I must go now. I'll be in touch with you, Kate. I'll write a note . . .'

'That'll be nice. Desmond will read it for me. That's Mr Maitland's name,' she said, again with that little trace of pride. Baba and Des—the two bright spots in her poor, tawdry life.

I should have felt some resentment that she had stolen the two men I loved, but I was numb. 'Yes, well, goodbye, Kate. It was—nice meeting you.'

'Grame told me so much about you. We'll keep in touch.'

Hotchkiss's knocking grew louder. I said goodbye and stumbled out the door. Loud recriminations rang in my ears as we hurried down the steep staircase. Hotchkiss had a deal to say about the fright I had given him. Ten minutes I had been gone, and such a parcel of ragamuffins had clustered around the carriage that he hadn't dared to leave it unattended.

I was still numb when he dispersed the boys and the carriage clattered over the road back to Elm Street. Graham was a father, though he had never seen his son. Kate must have conceived shortly before his death—about three months before. And he had been engaged to me at the time. So much for Eliot's assertion that the affair had happened long

212

before Graham had met me. He had juggled the two of us, mistress and fiancée. It was a terrible shock, but my former suspicions had helped to prepare me for the pain. It was of Desmond's treachery that I thought as the carriage pounded along.

He had gone darting off to Fleury Lane and had learned the story from Kate. He had sweet-talked the money out of her and had muddied the trail by pretending to believe that I had it. He had subjected my family to that ignoble search and had known all the time that we were innocent. It was perfectly clear why the neighborhood had been so unsuitable a place for me to visit. And he was still pestering me to reveal what Eliot and I were up to. He knew Eliot had been there once and feared he would return, too, for Kate had been warned not to let a man in. 'A lady' she thought it safe to entertain. In his generosity he had given her ten pounds and a promise to set her up in the country—to get her out of the city so no one would learn the truth.

Where should I go with my knowledge? Bow Street seemed the likeliest place, but I wouldn't go alone. I needed moral support. Mama? No, she would hate it. Eliot? Wouldn't he crow 'I told you so!' And so he had. He had warned me away from Fleury Lane and Mr Maitland. I wished I had heeded him. Regret clung to me like a shadow as we retraced our path to Elm Street. But it wasn't a shadow; that requires a source of light, and there was no light in this dark business.

CHAPTER THIRTEEN

I had not taken the precaution of forbidding Mama and Esther to go out. Ettie told me Mrs Mailer had called and was driving them to Bond Street. Once I had determined there were no gentlemen in the carriage, I was happy they were out of the house, as it gave me privacy to settle the unsavory Maitland business. I chose Eliot as my protector, mainly because his groom was to arrive shortly to remove the carriage. I would order Eliot off to Bow Street to report the affair. I took some cold comfort in imagining Mr Maitland in the dock, revealed as the scoundrel he was.

What charges would they lay against him? Stealing? But recovering your own money is not illegal, and he would doubtless claim that he meant to give Pelty his share. Leading poor Kate Norman astray? That would hardly land him in jail, or half the male population of London would be behind bars. Graham himself would be, if he weren't buried. There had to be something! It wasn't possible a man could behave as badly as Maitland had and not be held legally accountable for it. But my best efforts at conjuring up an indictable offense brought only frustration. He would get off scot-free to ruin other women and pester other law-abiding ladies.

Eliot's groom received the brunt of my humor when he arrived late to take the carriage away. 'I told you one hour!' I scolded.

'I was here an hour ago and waited in the kitchen till I was led out the door,' the saucy fellow replied in the most insolent way imaginable.

'I want you to go to Mr Sutton at once and ask him to come here. It is a matter of utmost urgency. And don't dawdle along the way.'

He did not verbally acknowledge my order but turned an impudent shoulder on me and ambled from the room. I thought he had moved swiftly in spite of his bold show, however, when Eliot arrived at the door within fifteen minutes.

'That's a nasty piece of merchandise you've hired to run your stable, Eliot,' I chided him. 'I never saw a more rag-mannered boy.'

'City servants are impossible,' he agreed. 'What did you think of the team I got for you?'

'They're fine, but that's not why I sent off such an urgent summons. Eliot, I've been to Fleury Lane.'

He made an involuntary jerk toward me, and his eyes grew wide with dismay. 'What? Belle, I told you not to go there.'

'Don't dismay yourself, Eliot I wasn't harmed.'

He settled into a disparaging smile. 'Then you've seen how Kate Norman and her sort live. Not a pretty sight. I only misled you to spare you the pain of discovery, Belle. You must not think too badly of Graham. It is regrettable, but many fellows do the same. If you had met Kate, you would have seen that at least she is a genteel soul, not vulgar and common as so many women of that sort are.'

'Genteel? That was not my impression!'

He started up from his chair. 'But surely you didn't meet her! I told—I was told she had moved to the country when I stopped at Fleury Lane. Oh, dear, then you know about the child. I had hoped to spare you *that,* at least. Still, you must have wondered why Graham bought such a small house for himself. It was the other family he had to provide for, of course, that necessitated it. I tried to talk him out of it, but you know Graham. He introduced me to the girl once—I don't know what he saw in her.'

I waved these details aside. 'It is all a hum that she's moved to the country!' I exclaimed, and had the pleasure of outlining the true story for him. He was nonplussed. 'I didn't think you would be so surprised. You told me all along Maitland had the money.'

'Yes, Belle, but I had no idea Miss Norman was involved.'

'She is innocently involved. Maitland is paying her off with ten measly pounds and the promise of a house in the country, with himself playing her protector. His aim is to remove her from the city so Pelty won't learn about her, of course. At the very least I mean to write Mr Pelty a note and report on Maitland. I wish I could see him behind bars.'

'He's shifty as a snake. Pelty will stick by him in the end. You'll see. It is a waste of time to bother going to Bow Street, though I should, perhaps, warn Miss Norman.'

'Poor Miss Norman. What will become of her and the child?' This had been bothering me, and a plan of action had begun to form. It was a radical one, but right.

'It's generous of you to worry about her! She'll land on her feet. Her sort always do, and she has youth and beauty on her side for a few years.'

'I have determined to help her in some way. Financial help, I mean.'

'Fifty guineas, perhaps . . . And I'll kick in the same amount, for Graham's sake.'

'That is kind of you, but a hundred guineas won't see a boy reared and educated. You will think I've run mad, but I mean to do more—a great deal more.'

He looked at me uncertainly. 'How much . . .'

'Everything Graham left me. The house—I can't bear the sight of it since I have learned the truth. He ought to have left it to his child, Eliot, not to me.'

'No, really, this is too much! You're

agitated. Think about it for a few days.'

'No, I'm afraid I'll change my mind, and I know this is the proper thing to do.'

'She wouldn't be at home in a neighborhood such as this.'

'I know that,' I agreed, with a wistful memory of the story of her being run out of the West End. 'I'll sell the house and set the money up in a trust for her, giving her an income that she can't be bilked out of. She is such a naive, gullible girl, it is the only thing to do. Perhaps she could buy a little cottage in the country. She seemed to like that idea.'

'It wouldn't take all the money Graham left you.'

I shook my head. 'Eliot, I expected better of you. This is Graham's son we are speaking of—your cousin.'

'Damme, who is to say Graham was the father?'

'Oh, if you had seen the child, you would not say that. He is the image of his father.'

He frowned and considered the matter. 'That's true. I haven't seen the child. There was no one home when I went. The old lady downstairs told me they had moved.'

'That would be because Mr Maitland had hustled her off to the country to look for a cottage. He won't keep his promise, though. I am the proper one to look after her, as a duty to Graham. Do you think he knew—about his son, I mean?'

218

'Yes, he knew. It troubled him greatly. That is the only reason he went on seeing her after your engagement.'

'The child was conceived after the engagement, Eliot. It is no longer necessary to spare my feelings. I want Kate to know her future is secured, and I want to warn her away from Maitland. Will you come with me to tell her so?'

'Let me do it for you. There is no need for you to go back. It must be painful for you. In fact, as you said, the child is my cousin. Why don't you appoint me its guardian? In that manner we can be assured Kate won't do something foolish with the money.'

'I want to talk it over with Mama, but it sounds a good idea. You will know about proper schooling for the boy and so on.'

We were both eager to get on with it, and Eliot left very soon after to call on Miss Norman. It was sad to know I was no longer an heiress, but I would never have had a moment's pleasure from the money, knowing Kate's straitened circumstances. Now she had a chance, and if there was any character in her, she could have a decent life. I thought she was young enough to make something of herself and Baba.

These were my thoughts as I sat alone, awaiting Mama's return. I would give Yootha a piece of my mind if she came in. She was as bad as Maitland. Maitland, who, alas, was still

Desmond in my secret thoughts. How could he be so treacherous? But he had behaved with unmitigated duplicity since the moment I had first laid eyes on his handsome face. He had always weaseled his way back into favor, but this time there would be no cajoling. Just last night he had spoken of our having trust in each other. It stung, he said, that I thought he was out to bilk Pelty. He'd probably been doing it for years! What had stung him was that he had finally fallen under suspicion. This would be enough to make him lose his license at Lloyd's, and I was vengeful enough that I meant to make sure Lloyd's was aware of his scheme.

I had just drawn out paper and pen to write to Mr Pelty, care of Lloyd's of London, when the door knocker sounded. Everything reminded me of Desmond, even the door knocker, which he had put on crooked. What a fine, genial gentleman we had all thought him that night.

Hotchkiss answered the door, and soon I heard the unmistakable accents of Mr Maitland in the hall, making some joke about the weather. Hotchkiss, who remained in ignorance of my findings at Fleury Lane, welcomed him like a long-lost friend.

I flew to the doorway to have Maitland ejected, but I was too late. He already had his hat off and was removing his coat.

'Don't bother undressing, Mr Maitland. You won't be staying,' I said.

That caused him to open up his eyes. He stood regarding me, a question on his face. 'What is it, Belle?' he asked.

I let him enter the saloon and waited till Hotchkiss had returned to the kitchen before delivering my tirade. 'I have been to Fleury Lane and met Kate Norman, Mr Maitland.'

He looked uncertain and finally said, 'Pretty little thing, isn't she?'

'She is to your liking? It doesn't surprise me. Have you actually taken her under your protection, then? I was sure it was a ruse to get her out of London.'

A doubtful, uneasy smile flickered briefly, petering out in a question. 'I beg your pardon?'

'I know everything. There's no need to walk on eggs. I daresay it is not illegal to recoup your money, or even to seduce that poor, ignorant girl, but I would advise you most strenuously to make sure Mr Pelty receives his share of the blunt. I was just writing a note to inform him that you have recovered the funds.'

'I beg your pardon?' he repeated.

'Don't bother. My pardon is withheld. I cannot condone your manner of doing business.'

He threw his hands out and stared incredulously at me. 'Belle, what in hell's name are you talking about? I haven't seduced anyone, and if you know who has my money, I wish you would tell me.'

My thin veneer of patience broke, and I shouted like a harpy. 'Don't bother lying to me! I tell you I know the whole squalid story. How you went chasing after that girl, got the money from her, hustled her out of town. You shouldn't have let her return. Oh, I know you directed her not to talk to anyone, but she mistook me for Graham's aunt, you see, and told me everything. I think you are a disgusting, contemptible cur. No, that's an insult to curs. You're worse—'

He took a step forward and clamped his hands on my upper arms. I was subjected to a severe shaking that left me winded. 'Get your hands off me, you vile creature!' I gasped.

'Will you please settle down and tell me what happened? I went once to Fleury Lane. I met Miss Norman and heard her story. I recognized her as the girl whose picture Sutton had under his pillow. She denied knowing anything about the money. I went back after that cut banknote turned up, and an old woman downstairs told me she had gone to the country. I admit Grant broke in and had a look around her flat. He found nothing. Are you telling me Miss Norman had the money all this time?'

'Are you telling me *you* didn't take it? She said she gave it to Mr Maitland, the insurance agent. She described you.'

He paced the floor, rubbing his chin. 'I didn't call myself Maitland.'

'Why not?'

'I don't know! I didn't want to frighten her, and if she had the money, the last person she'd tell about it was me. If she was criminally involved, I mean. How did she describe me?'

'Tall, handsome, jolly, dark hair . . .'

'Then it was him.'

I blinked in complete ignorance. 'Who?'

'Eliot Sutton. Belle, the reason I came here is to tell you I learned where Stone got that pound note. He was playing cards with Eliot and won. Eliot gave him three pound notes. One Stone must have given you, one was spent somewhere, and he still had the other. It was Eliot who went masquerading as me in Fleury Lane.'

'Oh, my God! It can't be!' I was shaken at the possibility, yet not unwilling to believe it. I looked hopefully for confirmation.

'Of course it is, and he got the money from that credulous girl by pretending it belonged to him.'

'But how would he know . . . ?'

'Didn't you direct him to her, as you directed me?'

'We discussed her.'

A look of deep aggravation settled on Desmond's countenace. He looked ready to throttle me. 'I thought we were going to trust each other. You actually believed me capable of behaving—'

It seemed the judicious moment to distract

223

him with more bad news. 'Des, he's with her now. I told him about you . . . I mean what Kate told me about Mr Maitland. What will he do?'

'You idiot! He'll kill her! He's already killed once for that money. How long ago did he leave?' He was darting for the door as he spoke, and I not a step behind him.

'Not long—fifteen minutes.'

He rammed his hat on his head, grabbed his coat, and pulled the door open. He stopped only long enough to push me back inside. I heard the door knocker fall off with the force of the door slamming. His groom already had the horses whipped into motion, and I saw Des running along beside the carriage, opening the door, and clambering in as the pace picked up.

I wandered in a daze back to the saloon and sank on the sofa to try to organize my muddled thoughts. To add to my confusion, I was aware of a rising joy that Des was exculpated—again. It was Eliot who had tricked Kate Norman, and I who had led him to her. And he had sat there with that sanctimonious face throughout my story to hear just how much I knew. But Des had accused him of even worse than this. *'He's already killed once for that money.'* Killed his own cousin.

How had he engineered it? He had known Graham's plan to recover the funds. I remembered Yootha saying he had tried to talk Graham out of it. He claimed to have been out of town that night, but he recognized that as a suspicious alibi. He had held the same thing against Des. He had even known what waistcoat Graham wore that night—how would he know that if he hadn't seen it? He had let Graham take all the risks while he sat waiting for him, right in this house. How had he gotten in? Did he have a key? The open cellar window—he might have opened it himself. He was often down there with Graham, arranging the wine racks. My skin crawled as I thought of the cold-blooded planning that had gone into his crime. And he had done this to his cousin and best friend! After that monstrous betrayal, he could accept Graham's watch as a token of affection and use it, carry it in his pocket. He valued it equally for the 'owner and the donor,' he had said. I knew then how high I stood in his esteem. He would have killed me without blinking if I hadn't been of use to him. How eagerly he had offered to be the guardian of Kate's money. He planned to bilk her out of it.

Maybe even kill her, Des thought. And if he planned to kill Kate, it wasn't likely he'd stop at killing Desmond, if he arrived in time to catch him. Did Des have a gun? I was up from the sofa, cursing myself for not having kept the carriage standing by. I'd have to run into the street and try to find a hackney. I grabbed my pelisse and ran like a frightened deer, gathering some very odd looks from ladies and gentlemen out for a stroll. I nearly capsized Mrs Seymour and her husband, and I hadn't time to stop and apologize. She shouted after me as I careered along to the corner, waving my arm to attract a cab's attention. Two drove past as though I were invisible.

I determined I would stop the next private carriage that came along. I was in the road waving, and it was an unexpected piece of luck that Ralph Duke was the first one to come by. He was coming to call on Esther, driving a sporting curricle. He jerked to a stop and stared at me. 'Good day, Miss Haley,' he said in a questioning voice.

I vaulted up on the perch beside him. 'Drive to Fleury Lane,' I ordered.

'Eh? What would you want to go there for, Miss Haley?'

'Never mind, just whip those nags up and drive.'

'Well, if you say so. Sure you wouldn't prefer the park?'

'Quite sure.'

'Er—Fleury Lane—not sure I know exactly where it is.'

'Near Long Acre.'

'I don't know that part of London.'

'East—drive east.'

'But I don't know that—'

I pulled the reins from him and we were off, and a very bizarre team we made, to judge from the stares bestowed on us as we rattled along. My having forgotten to don a bonnet might have had something to do with it, I daresay. It certainly played havoc with my hairdo.

'We really ought to switch to my closed carriage,' he suggested. 'I could have it brought around in—'

The horses were bolting dangerously, so I returned the reins to him. 'Just be quiet and drive. Turn left here. Can't you go any faster?'

'This is a city team, miss.'

'Give them the whip.'

'Maybe you'd care to take the reins yourself, Lady Lade.'

'Don't be impertinent!' I said coldly, though I hadn't a notion what he meant.

After a few false turns I espied Fleury Lane and directed Duke down it. I saw only Desmond's carriage standing in the street, but it was hardly reassuring. If Eliot had come with mayhem in mind, he wouldn't have left his rig there to be seen.

'That looks like Des's rig!' he exclaimed. 'Now, what the deuce would he be doing here?'

I turned to hop down from the perch, and Duke looked around for a boy to hold the reins.

'Wait here! I want you to wait for me.'

I didn't want his two left feet making a racket on the stairs. 'I think I should go with you. I mean to say—'

'Wait. I won't be long.'

I jumped down and ran toward the blue door. The bitter taste of fear was in my throat. My heart hammered painfully and my breath was short. What scene would await me? Eliot with blood on his hands, or a gun in them? I needed a weapon. I looked at Duke's whip, but I wanted something more manageable. I ran to Des's carriage, hoping to find a gun in the side pocket. All I found was another bottle of wine. I hefted it and deemed it heavy enough to knock Eliot out if I gave it a hard swing. With the bottle concealed under my pelisse, I returned to the blue door. I didn't knock this time but crept in and up those steep, dark stairs as quietly as a mouse, with my ears cocked for sounds of violence.

Kate's door was closed, and no shrieks or sounds of gunfire came through it. As I drew nearer I heard the wail of a distressed Baba. His crying overrode the quieter hum of adult voices. I first placed my ear against the door, and when this told me nothing new I put my eye to the keyhole. All I saw was a dark wall at close range. After a moment, I realized I was looking at the back of a man's blue jacket. Either Des or Eliot was standing a yard from the door, facing the room. The child stopped crying, and the buzz of voices cleared to recognizable words.

'Don't even think about it or she's dead, and the kid, too,' Eliot said. He shifted aside, and I caught a partial view of Kate from the shoulder down. She held the baby in her arms and was standing right in front of Eliot. Her fingers moved convulsively, making it easy for me to imagine her fear. Eliot was using the mother and child as a shield to get out of the room. Des must have a gun, then. 'Kate, get his gun. Put the kid on the floor, right here at my feet. If you want him back alive, you won't try anything.'

Kate made a low moaning sound, like a dying animal, but did as he said. She handed Eliot the gun and picked up her baby again. 'That's fine. That's just fine,' Eliot purred. Knowing him for what he was, I thought that purr sounded as menacing as the cocking of a pistol. He wouldn't leave them alive to report on him. He'd shoot Desmond first, then Kate.

Much good a bottle of wine would have done when he came out that door and saw me! I lifted the bottle and stared at it, regretting it was not a pistol. I would have to open the door and, try to crash the bottle against Eliot's skull before he turned around and shot me. I checked his position one last time and noticed that he had edged a step closer to the door. He wasn't more than eighteen inches from it now. I wouldn't be able to get it open without hitting him.

I couldn't see him raise his gun and take aim, but Kate's agonized wail told me that was what was happening. 'You can't . . .' she

229

whined. Of Desmond I saw nothing, not so much as an inch. Eliot's hateful back blotted him out entirely. By the time I saw him he'd be dead on the floor. The image rose up in my mind, showing me what would happen if I didn't move fast.

If I couldn't knock Eliot out with the bottle, I'd hit him with the door and knock him off balance I clutched the handle and pushed the door fast and hard, with all my might. It opened ten inches, met resistance, then suddenly gave way, and I nearly fell into the room. My first glance was to Desmond. He was alive—looking very like a ghost, but alive. While I stood staring, he moved forward, quick as a lizard. At my feet Eliot sprawled, still clutching the gun, with Kate wedged beneath him. Baba had flown out of her arms and sat, stunned, halfway across the room. Des was already lunging for Eliot, but I was closer and got in the first crack. I lifted the wine bottle and brought it down across Eliot's skull with enough force to break the bottle. I doubt that hard head cracked as easily. Wine trickled down his noble brow and splattered his jacket, but he was unaware of it. He was completely unconscious.

There was a mad, incoherent scramble as Des pulled the gun from Eliot's fingers, Kate eased herself out from under his prostrate form and soothed the squalling baby, and I gave Eliot's leg a kick for good measure. My toe ached worse than ever.

Then Des turned to me, with the gun dangling from his fingers, and asked in a shocked voice, 'What are you doing here, Belle?'

Witless with shock, I said, 'I just came. Duke brought me.' A smile trembled on his lips. He pulled me into his arms and said, 'I love you.'

I pushed him away. 'I bet you say that to everyone who saves your life.'

He took a long look into my eyes before speaking and reached for my hands. 'No, only to you.'

'I wish you'd put that gun down before you shoot someone.'

When we had all ascertained that none of us was mortally hurt, Des asked for ropes to bind up Eliot. I suspected that he had regained consciousness, but he played dead rather than face our wrath and contempt. When he was safely bound I hobbled downstairs to send Duke off to Bow Street. Before I could argue him into going, Bow Street came to us. Desmond had sent his groom there before coming to Fleury Lane, and we all went up to 2B.

'That looks like Eliot Sutton!' Duke exclaimed. 'Dead, is he?'

'We should be so lucky!' I answered.

'What happened to him?'

'I hit him over the head.'

'Ah.' He stepped back a pace, beyond my reach. 'You should have asked me for my pistol, Miss Haley. I was just coming from Manton's, and I have a brace of them in my curricle. But then, you wouldn't need a pistol,' he decided.

'No, I usually kill people with my bare hands, Duke.'

He backed away another step before he realized I was joking. Soon Officer Roy took charge, but it was an Officer Roy grown gracious to atone for his former rudeness. His condescension when Desmond explained events was hardly less repulsive than his other mode.

'So this brave little lady has saved the day, eh?' He beamed and patted my arm.

'Regular Turk,' Duke informed him.

'I knew you wasn't the sort to put up with any shilly-shallying,' Roy said aside, and gave me a wink. 'Knocked him galley west with the door, there's the ticket.'

'Get this carcass out of here as soon as possible. We have to clean up this mess,' I told him, and went to get the broom to sweep up the broken glass before Baba and Duke got into it, for Duke had taken control of Baba and was playing with him on the floor.

When I came back Roy had turned his revolting charms on Kate. He was making much ado over Baba, trying to wrest him from Duke's clutches in such a rough way that Kate soon removed her precious child to the bedroom.

'There's a pretty wee armful,' Roy said to Des, looking after Kate's retreating form. 'Is this her husband we're hauling away?' he asked. There was an undeniable glint of scheming in his eye as he considered that this left Kate unattended.

'No, she don't have a husband, Roy,' Des told him. There was an answering glint of understanding and approval in the look Des gave him.

'Eh, how does it come she has a kid, then?' Duke demanded. I was happy to see this token of conventionality in his thinking.

'Of that ilk, eh?' Roy asked, but in no disapproving way. It was only interest he displayed. 'A lass like that should have done better,' he added, glancing around the room. He took up one end of Eliot's body, Desmond's groom the other, and their conversation continued over the inert and sagging form. 'The lass,' Roy said 'Your bit of stuff, is she?'

Desmond, with unsteady lips, disclaimed any personal interest in the Incomparable. Before Roy left, he called down the hall to Kate, 'I'll be back shortly, miss. Around teatime.'

Kate came into the saloon and blinked a watery smile at him. 'Oh, thank you. It will feel so safe to have an officer in the house. They

233

won't lock me away, will they?'

'For what?' Roy asked, bristling up most impressively. 'The law hasn't sunk to locking up innocent victims yet. Not while Arthur James Roy has anything to say about it.'

'Oh thank you, sir.' She glowed. I'm sure Roy would have dropped Eliot and declared himself on the spot had it not been for his audience.

'Don't you worry, lass. I'll not be letting anything happen to you,' he promised, and backed out the door. 'You'll come along to headquarters, Mr Maitland, to lay charges?'

'I'll be right there,' Des replied, then turned to me. 'You'd best go home, Belle. I'll leave my groom here to give Kate a hand. Till her officer returns,' he added softly, with a little smile. 'An ill wind that blows no good, they say.'

'I'll stay with her.'

'Won't your mother be worried?'

'Yes, and it will do her a world of good to worry about me for a change.'

'Kate will be all right. I'd feel better knowing you were home.'

'Perhaps you're right. I have some business to tend to.'

'I'll stop by later. You *will* let me in, won't you?' he quizzed.

'That depends on what new developments occur. If I learn in the meanwhile that I've been wrong again, you may find the door blocked.'

'I think this time we've sorted it out, except to learn what he did with the money.'

Kate came to thank us. 'It was lucky you turned up when you did, Mrs Mailer,' she told me.

Duke gave a heavy frown and said, 'She ain't Mrs Mailer.'

Des opened his lips to explain, but it would have been such a long story that he decided to wait till later. Roy was hollering from the bottom of the stairs for him to come along. I stayed only till the groom returned to bear Kate company, then Duke said, 'Shall I take you home, Mrs Mailer?'

'Yes, please.'

'To which house, Elm Street or Berkeley Square?'

'I believe I'll go to my Elm Street address today, Duke.'

He gave me a questioning look but said nothing about my suddenly having become Mrs Mailer. 'What happened back there?' he asked.

'Nothing important. We scotched a snake.'

'You should have killed it,' he said, but soon twigged that Eliot was the snake in question. I explained the details of the matter and even invited him in when I returned home.

'You'll want to be alone with the family,' he said. 'This isn't the time for me to—interfere.'

A modicum of consideration was added to

Mr Duke's short list of credits. 'You're right, but do come back later, Mr Duke.'

'My name is Ralph, Mrs Mailer—er, Miss Haley.'

'My name is Belle, Duke.'

'An odd name for you.'

Must I now add wit to his credits? No, it was not intended as sarcastic humor, but only as a comment.

Before entering the house, I stood back and took a long look at it. It was difficult to imagine that but for an accident I would be the permanent mistress of this tiny establishment. My life would be circumscribed by Graham Sutton, his boring work, and his unsavory relatives and friends. I would be entertaining Eliot Sutton and Yootha Mailer. In time I might have come to accept their lax standards of propriety and their worthless daily routine. How very happy I was to have escaped it. I ran to the door, picked up the fallen brass knocker from the step, and went inside, smiling.

CHAPTER FOURTEEN

The short daylight hours of that November afternoon were fading to twilight before Desmond returned to Elm Street to give us his report. I had hoped for some privacy, but the little saloon was filled to overflowing. When

Yootha Mailer brought Mama and Esther back from their drive, she came in for a glass of wine. No sooner had they taken their seats than Mrs Seymour came over to inquire for the safety, and perhaps the sanity, of Miss Haley. Her reenactment of my flight in Duke's curricle was vivid enough that Yootha remained to discover its cause.

This made her late for an appointment with Mr Stone and Two Legs Thomson. The latter was experienced enough that he did not come looking for her, but Mr Stone tagged along to Elm Street. Duke had arrived about fifteen minutes after me and was there filling a chair and smiling at Esther.

After guiding Mrs Seymour to the door, I regaled Yootha with an account of her nephews' shenanigans. She emitted a few polite exclamations of disbelief and hastened on to what really interested her . . . 'You mean to say Miss Norman had the money all these years and wanted to give it to me?' It was as good as a raree show to watch the cunning greed on her face fade to regret.

I assured her that Graham had told Kate his aunt would come to collect it, and I demanded to know why she had abandoned the girl in her sorry plight.

'I had no idea she had the money!' she said.

'I suppose you had some idea she was enceinte, and totally destitute without Graham to care for her!'

'It was hardly *my* place to look after her! I don't believe in encouraging trollops. A woman like that—you may be sure she found some man to take her under his wing.'

As I had no idea how Kate had existed for those few years, my only answer was a blistering stare.

'But the child, Mrs Mailer!' Mama exclaimed. 'The baby is your great-nephew.'

'Rubbish! I don't intend to become a great-aunt for a good many years yet. I am much too young.'

'The poor girl,' Mama repined. 'Something must be done for her.'

'It is Belle who got the greater part of Graham's inheritance,' Yootha pointed out. 'If you feel so strongly that Graham's son requires support, it seems to me—'

'Naturally I shall provide for him,' I told her stiffly. She might as well have said she didn't believe me. Her glance said it as clearly as words would have.

Mr Stone shook his head and clicked his tongue. 'A waste of blunt, Miss Haley. Let the lithe beggar learn to fend for himself. It won't do him any harm.'

'Mr Stone!' Mama gasped, regarding him with the accusing eye of disillusionment. Mr Stone had just cured Mama of her temporary enchantment, and I was heartily glad of it.

When the wheels of Desmond's carriage were heard beyond the window Yootha

238

suddenly discovered it was time for her to go. 'You won't want to have much to do with that twisty fellow, Belle,' she warned me. They met at the door, both bowed stiffly, then Yootha and Mr Stone left as Desmond entered.

He made a much livelier tale of our afternoon than I had done. He substantiated my theory that Eliot had planned the whole theft well in advance and was lying in wait for Graham when he returned home that night with the money. 'He says he had no notion of actually killing Graham,' he said. 'He thought a black mask and a gun would be enough inducement to make Graham hand over the money. He reckoned without his cousin's determination. They got into a scuffle. Graham got the mask off him, and after that there was nothing for it but to do away with him. I can well imagine his chagrin when he discovered Graham didn't have the money with him.'

'Then it was Eliot who had been searching the house?' Esther asked.

'Half of London's been in and out. Eliot, my man Grant—I had a go at it myself, and I daresay Billie the Slash paid Elm Street a visit as well.'

'Billie the Slash?' Esther asked, blinking. 'What a horrid name! Does he slash people with a knife?'

'Not at all,' Des assured her. 'A slash is only a bullying, riotous cove. He's never hushed a

239

cull, to my knowledge.'

'Don't kill his mark,' Duke translated for her. 'So after Pelty posted the cole, Sutton snatched it and ran. Well, Des, you've whiddled the whole scrap now, eh? The stalling kens will do business with you again. That'll save you a few screens.'

'It's back to business as usual,' Des agreed.

'Did you recover your money?' Mama asked.

'Not yet, but Kate tells me Eliot took it to the cottage he hired for her just east of London. He was afraid to leave it in his flat, where I could easily have found it. I'm going to the cottage tomorrow. Some "wedding" Eliot was attending, eh?'

Mama nodded and said, 'If he hadn't made the mistake of letting Kate come back to the apartment in Fleury Lane, he might have gotten away with his scheme.'

'They always make one mistake,' Des said. 'Actually, Eliot made more than one. Once he began spending the banknotes I would have discovered the source eventually. He found Kate such a simple, biddable girl that he thought she'd follow his orders and not speak to anyone. He was in such a rush to get her out of Fleury Lane that he didn't give her time to pack up her belongings. She became quite insistent that Baba couldn't be happy without certain favored toys, and she herself had left behind some clothing and things. He brought her home to pack and was to pick her up again within an hour. His groom followed you this afternoon, Belle, and reported you'd been to Fleury Lane. Eliot was on his way to sound you out even before you sent for him.'

Mama sat listening with all the attention usually reserved for her reading of marble-covered novels. 'The poor girl. What a lot she has been through. Belle is going to do a little something for her.'

Thus far there had been no opportunity to divulge the extent of my charity, and the present moment was not opportune either, so I would reveal the truth later, when we were rid of our audience. Ettie's head appeared at the doorway, beckoning me.

'It's nearly time for dinner. Are they staying?' she asked.

They both agreed without so much as a token refusal. We dined informally, in our afternoon clothes. Dinner was merry, with the case our sole topic of conversation. I thought Mr Duke might have the grace to leave after dinner, but he had his sitting breeches on that night. We left the gentlemen to their port, and I outlined to Mama my intentions with regard to the house.

It took a little getting used to. 'Do you think—the *whole thing*, Belle?' she asked. I knew how she felt, but I knew too that a little deeper thinking would show her the rightness of my decision. Graham, though he was not the paragon I once imagined, had shown no evidence of abandoning his illicit family. He was by no means so dark a villain as Eliot. His whole plan to recover the money had been foolishly chivalrous, really. I expected an argument from Esther, for it was understood that my windfall would be shared by the whole family. She appeared completely uninterested.

'That is generous of you,' she complimented. 'I doubt I should give her *all* the money, if it were mine. Then you will be returning to Bath with Mama soon?'

'We shall *all* be returning!'

She colored up and agreed. 'That's what I meant, of course.' She didn't fool me for a minute. I knew now why Duke was sticking like a burr. Before the night was over, either Mama or I would be asked for her hand.

I think that without advice from Mr Maitland, Duke would have spoken to me. His wily mentor directed him to our more biddable mama and engineered the thing in such a way that I was left out of it entirely. Des came to the door and said, 'Mrs Haley, Duke would like to see you for a moment in the dining room.'

When she rose to go, I got up with her. 'Not you, Belle,' he said, taking hold of my hand.

Esther sat looking as innocent as a mouse in a cheese room. 'I have to get my embroidery,' she said, and darted from the room to listen at the keyhole. Esther had never embroidered a stitch in her life. She didn't even own a needle.

I ran after her. 'Esther, what have you arranged with Duke?'

'You'll see soon enough. And don't bother trying to talk me out of it, Belle. I'll marry him if I want to.'

'But you can't know you want to so soon! You hardly know the man.'

'I know him better than you knew Graham. At least he hasn't got a mistress and a by-blow stashed away in a corner. Besides, we don't plan to get married right away. He only wants permission to court me.' She left me without much to say, but it was clear she wanted my approval. 'You don't dislike him, do you?'

'I'm coming to like him better as I get to know him,' I admitted. Who was I to prate of 'not knowing' a man? Or of hasty engagements, for that matter? She had known him as long as I'd known Desmond. I hurried back to the saloon to discover if this betrothal business was contagious.

'I suppose you put Duke up to this,' I said to Desmond.

'It isn't a proposal, but only permission to court her.'

'Does he plan to remove to Bath?'

'If necessary. My half of the job is to convince you to remain on at Elm Street a little longer. Till Christmas, actually—only a month. We both thought Christmas a romantic time for an engagement.'

243

There was some little ambiguity in that 'both'.

To give us all time to become better acquainted,' he added blandly, and walked to the sofa.

'If Mr Duke has some hidden virtues, you must advise him to reveal them without delay.'

'His good nature is evident to the unprejudiced eye. He doesn't gamble; he's not a womanizer; he loves her. And she appears to return the honor. His little human failings need not concern you unduly. After all, you won't have to live with him. He's a sound man. What more can you want in a brother-in-law?'

'At least six inches! He's not as tall as I am.'

'He's taller than Esther. A man's value isn't measured in inches.'

I considered this unlikely gentleman as a brother-in-law and proceeded to the next matter of importance. 'He's well-to-do, at least, I believe you said?'

'A regular nabob. A baronial estate in Sussex and a mansion in Belgrave Square. You will have an opportunity to see the latter tomorrow, if all goes well, and the former at Christmas. He hopes to have you all there for the holiday.'

'Both' had become 'you,' not 'us,' and my spirits flagged accordingly. 'You spend the Christmas holiday in London, do you, Des?'

'No, I'm a near neighbor of Duke's in Sussex. That's how we became bosom beaux. I

244

hoped to induce you to visit me for New Year's. I usually have a ball. Liz and her husband will be with me for the season, or I would be joining Duke's party.'

This sounded interesting enough that I cast no more spokes in Duke's wheel. 'It is in Mama's hands. It is to her you should be telling these things, not to me.'

'Duke is telling her, if he is following my instructions. My job was to convince *you*, Belle. Are *you* interested?'

The glow in his eye denoted more than concern for Duke's success. 'I shall abide by my Mama's decision.'

'But before I speak to her, do you dislike the idea?'

'As long as Esther is happy . . .'

'My sweet shrew, I have just been telling you that the failings of a brother-in-law need not concern a lady unduly. I'll undertake to please Esther—it's your opinion we're discussing.' I revised the meaning of a few pronouns and understood that his speaking to Mama was on his behalf and my own, not Duke's. I listened in a trance as he continued. 'Could you be happy with a man who consorts daily with the ragtag and bobtail of society, and who occasionally serves you with a warrant? I will undertake to remove Grant from my household if you really dislike him.'

'No!'

His brows rose swiftly, and a stiffness

entered his body, requiring me to hasten on and make myself clear. 'I begin to understand Mr Grant's language. It won't be necessary for him to leave.'

The stiffness melted, and his arms folded around me like a warm blanket. His voice in my ear was ragged with relief. 'You gave me a bit of a turn there. Offering to dispense with Grant was the supreme sacrifice. He's my lifeline to Stop Hole Abbey. Between Grant and me, we'll have you pattering flash in no time.'

'Stubble it, Des.'

'Well spoken, moll,' he said, and lifted his head to smile at me. For a moment we gazed at each other in that witless-looking way lovers have. Des appeared quite bereft of common sense, and I knew I was smiling like a moonling, yet I couldn't stop. Far from being revolted by my expression, he crushed me against him for a merciless kiss. My blood quickened as his lips firmed in attack. I returned every pressure with unladylike force till my scalp tingled and my lungs felt ready to burst. Christmas suddenly seemed very far away.

'It's early to be asking you for a commitment,' Des said a moment later, 'but sometimes *later* doesn't come. It flashed into my head when I was looking down Eliot's gun muzzle that I was going to die and I had never told you I love you, Belle. That's why I told you at such an inopportune moment this afternoon. I don't need a year to make up my mind, and I think you're like me in that respect. At least, you seem capable of *hating* me at the drop of a hat, so your emotions must be easily engaged,' he added, quizzing me with a smile.

A bustling in the hallway announced that the others were joining us, and we jumped to our feet in guilty haste. It would be hard to say which smile was broader, but I think Mr Duke won the day. His smile dwindled as he caught sight of me, but he came forward manfully for my congratulations.

'You're saddled with me now, Miss Haley,' he said, rubbing his palms against his trousers to remove the perspiration before touching me. Something in my face told him he was safe. He laughed, and instead of shaking my hand, he reached up and placed a brotherly smack on my chin, then jumped back, astonished at his own daring.

'Am I to congratulate you, Des?' he asked.

'She got me,' was Des's refined way of announcing my capitulation.

'She has agreed to consider an offer,' I explained.

I felt a little sorry for Mama, who was left out in the cold. We broke open a bottle of Graham's champagne and discussed our future, the only bone of contention being which of us should have the pleasure of

Mama's company, though she was much inclined to return to Bath alone.

'Well, girls, the trip didn't work out so badly after all, did it?' Mama asked happily. She would have had to go some length to outdo herself on that understatement!

This and other details were to be worked out later. Des claimed his aunt was still interested in my house, and there was a lawyer to consult about arranging Kate Norman's trust fund. It seemed December would be busy, but not busy enough to preclude our courting.

The little house on Elm Street would ring with much merry joy, and I sincerely hoped that Desmond's aunt, or whoever bought the house, would be as happy in it as I was at that moment. I knew I would never have been a tenth as happy with Graham. I had learned to forgive him—how could I not, when he was indirectly the cause of my good fortune? I would forgive and then forget. It was time to bury the past and start a new leaf.

Chivers Large Print Direct

If you have enjoyed this Large Print book and would like to build up your own collection of Large Print books and have them delivered direct to your door, please contact **Chivers Large Print Direct**.

Chivers Large Print Direct offers you a full service:

✧ **Created to support your local library**

✧ **Delivery direct to your door**

✧ **Easy-to-read type and attractively bound**

✧ **The very best authors**

✧ **Special low prices**

For further details either call Customer Services on 01225 443400 or write to us at

Chivers Large Print Direct
FREEPOST (BA 1686/1)
Bath
BA1 3QZ